Diamond in the Rough

Reiki Under Fire

Grateful Steps Foundation
159 South Lexington Avenue
Asheville, North Carolina 28801

Copyright © 2013 by Dale Stacy
Library of Congress Control Number 2013940102
Stacy, Dale
Diamond in the Rough
Reiki Under Fire
ISBN 978-1-935130-64-2 Paperback

Cover design by Sundara Fawn

Printed in the United States of America
at Create Space
FIRST EDITION

www.gratefulsteps.com

For Jeanne, Laura & Luci

Acknowledgments

Many thanks to Micki Cabaniss Eutsler and the amazing team at Grateful Steps in Asheville, North Carolina, for their tireless efforts, guidance and support. Micki took a rough draft of an idea and made a dream come true. It is truly a blessing to work with kindred spirits who have a passion for the written word.

To Simone Lipscomb and Laine Cunningham, thank you for your support, suggestions, editing and friendship. You are truly diamonds in the sky as you light the way for others.

To my many friends in the law enforcement field, thank you for what you do and for educating me in the ways of the warrior.

Many thanks and hugs to our friends who are part of EarthStar Spiritual Center. Your support and love have kept me afloat with your constant encouragement and participation in spiritual endeavors.

And finally, for my soulmate, whose eyes sparkle like sunbursts each and every day, my wife, Jeanne. Thank you, my love. What an adventure we live together! I hope for many more to come.

This is a fictional story. All the characters, organizations and persons in this novel are a product of the author's imagination. If real names or titles appear, they are solely for use in a fictional sense without any intent to describe their real purpose.

Five Principles of Reiki

1. Don't get angry today.
2. Don't worry today.
3. Be grateful today.
4. Work hard on your spiritual self today.
5. Be kind to others today.

Diamond in the Rough

Reiki Under Fire

Dale Stacy

Grateful Steps Foundation
Asheville, North Carolina

CHAPTER 1

THE UNLIT ROOM exploded with the yellowish flicker of the match as the air filled with sulfur. Dalilah lit her much-needed cigarette, even though she told herself she wasn't a smoker. She concentrated on her breath, listening as she sucked in air to bring the ember to life. She did it just because she wanted to and because it relaxed her.

The light shining from the match bounced off her face. High cheekbones, full red lips and flowing brownish-black hair made her a striking and attractive woman. Her real beauty, though, rested deep within, along with a heart yearning for that special connection—for the love she knew had to exist.

She was alone. Divorces were never easy. Once again the love she needed, hoped for, demanded and deserved, had eluded her. She was a good person, kind to old people and animals, a good tipper, a courteous driver, a gentle soul. But love always seemed beyond her grasp. At times she felt she was very close. Then just at the last moment, it would vanish. Perhaps she was struggling with fate or karma. For now she hadn't a clue. For now she really didn't care. She toyed with the diamond necklace draped just at the furrow of her cleavage. The necklace brought back memories—she had been so close to having it all.

Dalilah picked up the phone and dialed his number, hoping he was there. Maybe he had found a change of heart. He could only give part-time love. And she couldn't accept partial love. It had to be all or nothing. But now perhaps any love was better than none at all. But it had to be on her terms. It had to be real. It had to be true. She deserved no less. The phone rang, and she felt the knots in her stomach as her palms became sweaty. Her heart beat faster.

A familiar voice answered, "Hello."

It wasn't his voice. It was her friend. A female friend. She put the phone down without speaking.

Now, she was pissed!

CHAPTER 2

THE NEXT MORNING Dalilah returned to her routine, the basic staples of any beautiful, hopeful, and daring woman of the new millennium—stale bagel with low-fat cream cheese and, of course, herbal tea. What a night! She thought she'd reconnected with her ex. She thought she'd seen something in his eyes, something different, even magical. But he had just wanted a nostalgic one-night stand, and he had even asked to borrow money. Still the same jerk. What lessons she had learned! Trust your instincts, Dalilah. Never settle. You deserve the best! But anyhow, it was too early in the day to have such a deep conversation with her Gemini self. Right now she just wanted to relax, drink her tea and practice Tai Chi.

She loved the deep breathing, the focus and the empowerment she felt during her Tai Chi practice. All that mattered at this moment was pure peace and harmony. The rest of the day might turn to hell; but for right now, it was a piece of heaven. To warm up, she started at her ankles and moved every joint until she finished her neck rotations. Then she gracefully performed Phoenix Spreads Its Wings—five breaths in and five breaths out, with arm movements up and down as if flying in slow motion.

Dalilah loved expanding her lungs with the primal calmness of dragon breaths. She loved the feeling of the life force—chi—as it coursed through every cell. It was instant euphoria with natural simplicity. She was grateful that her dad, a Tai Chi Master of Korean heritage, had taught her these wonderful movements. Tai Chi Chuan, supreme ultimate fist. If only love could come to her as easily as Tai Chi.

She began the 108 forms of Yang Style Tai Chi Chuan. Dalilah moved as a silk scarf in the wind, dancing effortlessly in blissful, mindless excellence. A casual observer would never guess she could kill with a single blow and that Tai Chi was a deadly martial art. She was a warrior. At this point in her life, she had never used Tai Chi in a real-life martial situation; she had no idea how far she would go to protect someone she loved.

Tai Chi was one way that Dalilah was able to maintain her strength and mind-body connection. Not only was she a thirty-something woman with exceptional intelligence and perspective, but her petite body had all the right curves with the muscular tautness of an Olympic gymnast. Dalilah's smooth skin was without flaw, and the olive complexion inherited from her father gave her a golden ambience. Her smile was genuine and infectious, and her soulful brown eyes sent out a constant twinkle to any soul mate capable of receiving the message.

As Dalilah completed her final bow, ending her Tai Chi practice, she surrounded herself in a ball of golden-white light. She exhaled one last deep breath and felt the peace of life everywhere.

After her shower, she knew it was time for work. Her father had also taught her some other things, mainly how to read people, and she was good at it. That's why she was one of the top private investigators in the country. Nobody could read people like Dalilah. Major corporations around the world courted her employment. But she chose independence and maintained her base of operations in Greensboro, North Carolina.

Everybody had a personal energy field, and people became magnetized to certain locations, people and things. Greensboro was her hometown. It felt right, and this was where she was supposed to be. At least for now.

CHAPTER 3

DALILAH PULLED OUT the top drawer of the file cabinet next to her desk and gave all the folders a cursory glance. She kept backup files at her home office just in case she wanted to review them late at night. The files represented five years of her life. It was not that she couldn't remember most of the information; she had perfect recall when she wanted to use it. Rather, she didn't want to remember.

Most of the information she gathered about people ruined their lives. Companies and individuals were willing to pay top dollar for information, mostly to discredit a business partner or competing corporation. She needed to work on creating a better quality of clientele. She felt she needed more substance, more truth and more nobility in her work. She wanted to make a difference. Dalilah listened to her inner voice and heard her dad, "Does your path have heart?" Dalilah opened a new information brief that had arrived yesterday, but her mind kept wandering to last night. She caught herself and focused on the new file. The same information broker from previous cases had sent her this particular inquiry. The broker preferred the word "inquiry." It sounded softer than "investigation."

Given the source, Dalilah knew a rich sponsor had funded it. Someone wanted this information badly, and he wanted it quickly. Three $$$ signs were stamped at the top of the information sheet. This was a code her broker used to signify the immediate need for the information. One $ sign was the usual corporate job. Two $$ signs meant an individual needed an above-average response time, and he or she was willing to pay extra for the service. Three $$$ meant drop everything else and expect a significant bonus for the speedy results.

Dalilah would deliver as promised.

CHAPTER 4

RIVING TO THE office in her candy-apple red Chrysler Sebring convertible and listening to NPR for her morning news report, she saw a dark sedan in her rearview mirror. Have I picked up a tail? She was always wary, but she hadn't been followed in quite a while. Recalling her training from her dad, a retired police detective, Dalilah began evasive maneuvers. She changed lanes, slowed down and sped up. So did the mysterious car.

Dalilah did what any trained detective would do—she initiated a Batman turn by stepping on the emergency brake with a hard turn of the wheel to the left, causing the car to spin 180°. It was a perfect execution; but she found herself in the middle of traffic, headed the wrong way on a one-way street. She dodged the oncoming traffic amidst the agitated symphony of blaring car horns. As the dark car passed, she glanced back to her left and saw the plate—JHS-803. A glare on the window prevented her from seeing the driver. She quickly turned onto a side street, picked up her cell phone and made a call to her godfather, who still worked for the police department.

"Uncle Kyle, this is Dalilah. I need a favor."

Kyle replied, "What's the tag number?"

In police phonetics, Dalilah read off the number: "John Henry Sam 803, black sedan, maybe a Crown Vic."

Kyle told her he'd call her back ASAP. It was the least he could do for his goddaughter, especially since he'd been there the day she'd been born in the back of a squad car. Her dad had been on a special undercover assignment and had missed the birth.

Dalilah slowed down and checked her rearview mirror to see if the driver had any perseverance. No one was in sight. Then all of a sudden a black car shattered the silence of the morning as it exited from a nearby alley. Dalilah saw something shiny in the man's hand as he held it outside the window. It was a gun. Dalilah turned her car around and stomped on the gas pedal, only to have the car lurch forward in a choking stall. She tried to crank the car as she noticed the gas light on her console. She had forgotten she was running on empty.

As a Gemini, she often forgot minor details since her thought processes worked so fast. When most people were bogged down with details, Dalilah had bypassed them and moved on to the next thought. Dalilah knew she was a sitting duck, so she got out of the car and ran to the other side. She wanted the car's engine between her and the bad guy in case he decided to shoot. Pulling out her cell phone and maintaining eye contact with the car, she hit the speed dial for Uncle Kyle.

The phone rang. "Honey, you must be in a hurry."

"Uncle Kyle, 10-33, Elm and Bessemer, black sedan 10-32!"

"Hold on, Dalilah, I'll have a car there ASAP."

Kyle notified police communications of an emergency—suspect armed. Dalilah could hear the sirens as police cruisers came from every direction. But when they arrived, the suspect had already left the scene, having easily passed two responding vehicles.

Dalilah was leaning against a police car when Kyle saw her. He immediately rushed over to her and hugged her. Dalilah returned the squeeze.

"Sweetheart, the car following you is one of ours. Who did you piss off this time?"

"What do you mean, one of yours?"

"The car was stolen from the city garage last night, so I don't have a good feeling about this one. Tell me what you have."

Dalilah, possibilities exploding in her head, told him, "I don't have anything yet. Maybe it's related to a new case I just got. It's an anonymous job with bonus money for fast information."

"If you've given the officers all the suspect info, let me drive you to the office. I'm sure Liza will want to hear about this. By the way, why didn't you just outrun him in your car?"

"Well, I kinda forgot to fill up this morning."

"I thought your dad was just kidding with all that Gemini crap; but he was serious, wasn't he?"

"It happens to the best of us. Now, can we just go to my office?"

"Okay, Kid. I'll make sure the guys get your car towed to the gas station. Then I'll have it delivered to the parking garage."

"Thank you, Uncle Kyle. Thank you for everything."

Kyle pulled to the curb in front of Dalilah's penthouse office suite in the heart of downtown Greensboro. Jefferson Standard Life Insurance was the flagship corporation for the city, and its forty-two-story building made quite an impression silhouetted against the evening sky. The architecture of the building's apex ensured that anyone arriving in Greensboro for the first time would know immediately where the city's financial power lay.

When Dalilah first decided to base her business in Greensboro, she had wanted a premier location. Greensboro's nickname, the Gate City, was derived from its historical railroad roots and for being the gateway to commerce in Central North Carolina. This was her home, and she liked the rolling hills of the Piedmont region.

Dalilah got out of the car as Kyle, in his godfather voice, reassured her he would put out some feelers and check on the progress of the stolen police car. She kissed him on the cheek and thanked him again.

She made her way to the elevator, wondering if the new case had created all this excitement.

She pushed the button to the floor of EarthStar International. She had chosen the name because people got funny notions when it came to detective agencies, reminiscent of shady alleyway deals and scandalous divorce cases. Her dad, in fact, had been the one to suggest the name as it seemed ambiguous yet progressive.

Dalilah stepped off the elevator and felt that something wasn't right. With her martial arts training, countless nights on surveillance and meditative practices, she had learned to trust her keen intuition. It had never failed her. As she got closer to her office door, she found it ajar.

Entering, Dalilah heard shuffling noises in the back room. Reaching into her purse for her pepper spray, she approached quietly and found her confidant/secretary picking up files from the floor. Relieved, she said, "Thank God."

Liza, a competent, wise and elegant lady, had come to EarthStar after retiring as an administrative assistant in the police department's criminal investigation division. She knew everyone, so she practically ran CID. If you wanted to know anything, you just had to ask Liza. She was attractive, in her early fifties with blonde hair and green eyes. Her makeup was always impeccable, and she was very neat in both dress and demeanor.

Liza looked up. "Looks like somebody's interested in what we're doing. Any ideas yet, Ms. Smith?"

Even though Liza was older than Dalilah, she still called her Ms. Smith. She thought that it promoted a professional atmosphere for clients even though Smith wasn't Dalilah's real last name. "No, I haven't had time to really look at this new case. I guess I'd better make time. Is anything missing, or is someone sending us a message?"

Liza raised her eyebrows with a look of "who knows, business as usual" as she continued picking up papers, files and pictures. This wasn't the first time for this type of incident, and it probably wouldn't be the last. Their office had been burglarized before, but that had been an upset ex-husband—a case Dalilah had worked early in her career, right out of college.

The only thing that bothered Dalilah was that in her previous office, security wasn't very tight, so she could understand the breaking and entering there. But this building had state-of-the-art security with night watchmen and laser, heat and motion sensors. For Christ's sake, this building belonged to an international insurance company with impressive security, especially since 9/11. So whoever did this had slipped past the routine sweeps made by the security officers.

And the officers here were not rent-a-cops. All of these guys were ex-military or police officers working off-duty. With all the international corporations and financial data housed within the building, security was a main priority. Dalilah had thought this facility was the most secure location in the city. Apparently not. If the Jefferson Standard Insurance building could be compromised, then no place in Greensboro was secure.

Dalilah sat at her desk and leafed through the papers of the new brief. She focused her attention, looking for any unusual information. Meanwhile, one part of her brain rehashed her morning's activities—drinking herbal tea—followed by a stolen car—and a ransacked office.

She whispered to herself, "God, I love my life!"

CHAPTER 5

DALILAH SEARCHED THE contents of the brief with a driven fervor. She was quite an accomplished reader, speed-reader actually, a thousand words a minute. She was Phi Beta Kappa with a key. She had a double major from North Carolina State University—political science and international business. Her parents had paid for her college, so Dalilah never had to work those coed jobs—waiting tables, delivering pizza or serving in the quad's dining hall. All she had to do was study.

Her dad reminded her of that fact often. "School and studying are your job. Have fun and graduate soon. You have four years."

She rifled through the initial details and general aspects of the request. Upon taking a case from the "broker," she required that a summary and desired objectives be included in the material. According to the general information sheet, this client was a first-time user.

Her cases were always quite anonymous. Background information would be provided, along with any security or threat precautions. Payment for her services had to be made to the broker up front, along with the client's understanding that expenditures outside the normal range would be at additional cost. The broker was a very prestigious firm located in New York City. After completion of the job, Dalilah would receive payment in a timely manner. No questions asked. None of Dalilah's previous jobs had ever come close to being dangerous. Until now. Perhaps it was time to ask more questions and find out some details about her broker.

Dalilah continued reading. Apparently the information desired in this case had to do with international shipping, customs and diamonds. She loved diamonds; they were her favorite gemstone, in fact. Dalilah sang in a low voice, just like Marilyn, "Diamonds are a girl's best friend."

After reading the entire report, Dalilah had a better understanding of the case. It involved a multi-million dollar industry, perhaps even in the billions. Now she knew why she was being tailed and her office had been ransacked. It was definitely time to find out the source of the money for this investigation. Basic investigation 101 . . . follow the money.

That this particular client had lots of wealth was verified by the bonus attached to the brief. Her information broker's main office was in the Rockefeller Center in New York City. The firm was obviously on retainer with several international corporations and many governmental agencies. They were the information clearinghouse for planet Earth, and Dalilah was one of their top investigators.

Dalilah had been referred to them through a contact her dad had with an NYPD detective. When the broker needed information, she was contacted by a package shipped Fed-Ex overnight. Dalilah had worked several cases for the firm but never anything that raised so many intuitive flags. Its secrecy had the familiar nuance of industrial espionage, yet there was something else. Dalilah couldn't quite put her finger on it right now, but she would remain very cognizant of its existence.

The wheels turned in her head. She might need some outside help for this one. A close friend who worked for the Marine Patrol in Morehead City, North Carolina, could help with the port security and customs inspections. And she would call her college roommate who had an exclusive position with the diamond merchants' consortium in New York City.

It was time to call in some markers.

CHAPTER 6

A CAUCASIAN MALE driving a dark Ford sedan came to a stop on a dead-end street on the east side of Greensboro. He stepped out of the car and started walking, while removing his cell phone from his dark-colored suit jacket. Within two minutes a Yellow Cab stopped beside him.

"Starbucks. Battleground Avenue."

The cab driver nodded his head as they sped off to the other side of town.

The Ford would not last long in this neighborhood, especially with the keys still in the ignition. Some teenagers would find it and indulge in a joy ride. After all, kids will be kids, especially with the chance to drive an unmarked police car. They might provoke a chase with a marked police unit and videotape the event for their friends or do some high-speed driving on the Interstate until the gasoline runs out. At any rate, the stolen car would be stolen again. Fingerprints from the new car thieves would be all over the car. There would be no way to connect him to it.

The cab arrived at a shopping center with a health-food store, post office, karate studio and other retail businesses . . . not a minute too soon. Frankly, he was tired of hearing the hip-hop blaring in the cab. He told the driver to stop in front of the post office. The cabbie left with his obnoxious music—off to disturb someone else's otherwise perfect day.

Walking about a hundred yards to the other side of the parking lot, the man entered Starbucks. The aroma of freshly brewed Arabica beans wafted through the shop. Another man dressed in a sport coat and slacks entered from the side door and stepped up to the counter. Both men watched the young coed working with a hurried precision. With quick darting movements like a hummingbird in a feeding frenzy, she looked like an avid consumer of her employer's caffeine-laden beverages.

The man who had entered from the side door placed an order. "I'll have a Sumatra Grande, and leave room for cream."

The perky coed replied, "Yes, sir, Special Agent. Coming right up. Would you like a bagel, as usual?"

The man in the dark suit made a mental note.

CHAPTER 7

Detective Sergeant Kyle Steed was a twenty-eight-year veteran of the police department. He and Dalilah's dad were partners for ten years prior to her dad's early retirement. Kyle was a gentle man. His large frame of six-feet-three-inches and 250 pounds gave him the appearance of a giant. Most of his size was pure muscle. He still had the physique of the football player he was in college.

Although he was only in his early fifties, carrying a gun for a living had taken its toll. His dark hair was losing a battle against the wisps of gray surrounding his temples and moustache. Steed often exuded a playful sense with his boyish grin and a tendency to giggle. He often got lost in his own thoughts, as he was quite the philosopher, although few people took the time to listen to him.

Dalilah's dad was one who did. Probably the reason the two men were such good friends was that they understood each other.

Currently Sergeant Steed was in charge of the Fraud Squad in the Greensboro Police Department. The Squad's primary investigative focus was bad checks, forgeries, false pretenses, scams and credit card fraud. But with the increase in computer-related crimes, they had expanded their investigative skills into new criminal endeavors—child pornography, terrorist websites, international money laundering, identity theft and a growing host of information security violations.

Steed had finished his work for the day and decided to check with the Auto Squad detectives regarding the stolen police car that had followed Dalilah. No one had any new information. Out of curiosity and a gut feeling, he reviewed last night's duty roster. One name stood out.

Why was he working last night? Steed thought.

CHAPTER 8

DALILAH'S CLIENT WANTED information on diamonds, but not just any diamonds—Russian lab-created diamonds. According to the preliminary intelligence that accompanied the request, the market was being flooded with Russian-made diamonds. The broker always provided intel with his initial job request, which Dalilah found useful.

Although these diamonds were lab-created, they were supposedly flawless. Some jewelry store clerks, using a loupe or the 10x hand magnifier, couldn't detect the difference. They were perfect, a marvel of modern science, duplicating Nature even better than Nature.

Made of highly compressed carbon, diamonds are the hardest gemstone with the highest rating on the Moh's scale—a ten. Some of the lab diamonds were designed with inclusions, dark spots of carbon or other minerals that replicate "real" economy diamonds. The Russian scientists and venture capitalists had thoroughly researched this commodity. No expense had been spared to supply the demand of the world's market.

All tiers of the criminal world enjoyed a piece of this pie. The lowest rung, the street criminals, used slight-of-hand skills and posed as engaged couples shopping for a diamond ring. The typical M.O. targeted the finer jewelry stores where the couples perused loose diamonds for a custom-made ring. As they diverted the clerk's attention, the switch would be made.

If the clerk were a woman, the charming man created the distraction. With a male clerk, the perky fiancée provided the needed attention-getter with a low-cut top and push-up bra. The signal for a successful switch was a laugh. As soon as either partner heard a substantial laugh, the other knew the switch had been made. Before leaving, they would inform the clerk they were going to look around for the best price. The clerk was never the wiser. Only when the corporate gem auditor made the monthly visit would the scam be discovered.

However, since the fake diamonds were flawless, they would often be placed back into the case for sale as real diamonds. After all, stockholders are interested only in profit. So why disappoint the masses when no one knows the difference? Dalilah read this rhetorical part of the brief and said softly, "Who's the real criminal here?"

Dalilah continued reading. She finally got to the paragraph that stated the actual and specific request. For the first time she hesitated—a Russian holding company." *Could this be Russian Mafia?* She had wondered earlier why a hefty bonus fee had been offered for this case. Now she knew why.

CHAPTER 9

HE MEN WORKING the docks were tired. It was late, and it was cold. Although they had been born and reared in this small port town a few hours north of Moscow, they still complained about the cold winters. Work was scarce, and every job was necessary. It still didn't help the morale because everyone knew about the crates.

The crates were large, and the contents were quite grisly. Most of the markings on the containers were in Russian except for one panel in English, KEEP FROZEN – MEDICAL SUPPLIES. Bodies used by medical schools all over the world were shipped out every weekend, approximately one thousand per month. Most of the cadavers had been frozen for some time—casualties of war from the Balkan conflict.

Not all the victims of the war had been placed in mass graves. War was business. An expensive, money-making venture with guns, ammunition, tanks, airplanes, food and other supplies. And to the victor go the spoils, including corpses. Medical schools need bodies for research and classrooms. The bodies could not always be elderly people who donated their cadavers to science. There was a high demand for children, women and young men so the students could study a variety of body types.

Some of the corpses were a little different. They seemed to weigh more than the average medical cadaver. The young Russian dockworker opened the door to retrieve more bodies. The older supervisor had told him to remove only the bodies on the right side of the aisle tonight. He thought that quite odd; however, he was new at the job and did what he was told.

CHAPTER 10

DALILAH REACHED INTO her pocketbook and grabbed her cell phone to search the numbers she had stored. There he was—Brad Lewis, ex-Marine Corps Military Police. He had been stationed at Camp Lejeune in Jacksonville, North Carolina. She dialed Brad's number in Morehead City.

Brad was now an officer for the Marine Patrol, part of the North Carolina Department of Environmental and Natural Resources. The Marine Patrol was responsible for monitoring the harvest of the state's fisheries, along with patrol duties, including piers, beaches and all waterways up to three miles offshore. Basically, it was a brother organization to the Highway Patrol. Brad was a trooper on the water.

With the tightened security atmosphere in America, the Marine Patrol had a new mandate with Homeland Security. Working in close conjunction with the U.S. Coast Guard, the Patrol also prevented terrorists and hazardous materials from entering U.S. shores through local ports and beaches. But as with most governmental agencies, the Marine Patrol had a limited budget for an impossible job.

Brad answered, "Sergeant Brad Lewis, Marine Patrol."

"How are you doin', good lookin'?" Dalilah said. "I was wondering if you could help me. I seemed to have misplaced my pet dolphin. Any recent reports concerning its whereabouts?"

"Dalilah, is that you? Are you in town? Cause I'd love to see you, sweetheart."

"No, Brad. I'm in Greensboro, but I'm headed your way in about two hours. Will you be free this evening?"

Brad replied the same as any young-blooded single male with the chance to have dinner with a positively beautiful, sexually uninhibited and unattached goddess. "I am now. Why don't you meet me at my place, and you can freshen up while I cook dinner?"

With an impish grin, Dalilah said, "I'll see you at 6:00."

CHAPTER 11

DETECTIVE SERGEANT KYLE Steed heard the door open in CID. He peered over the partition of his cubicle and saw Special Agent Rickard walk in. Steed didn't like Rickard, but he was on temporary assignment with the Criminal Investigation Division as part of a federal task force to apprehend violent offenders. It was a way for local police agencies to receive government grants and to share in the new-found cooperation among federal, state and local jurisdictions. Since 9/11 there was a call to arms among law enforcement agencies to re-ignite the brotherhood, in the interest of national security.

Sergeant Steed approached Rickard's desk. "I understand you were working last night?" Rickard stiffened. He was a federal officer and not accustomed to answering to local police about his duty schedule. "Yes, I did work last night. Why? You writin' a fuckin' book or something?" Sergeant Steed bristled, but responded coolly, "No, I was just wondering if you heard about the unmarked police car being used in a joyride this morning. It was stolen from the garage on Patton Avenue."

"Actually I didn't hear about it until this morning. I was having coffee at Starbucks. Channel 2 news."

Even though he didn't care for Rickard very much, he was a sworn officer, so he showed him common courtesy and said, "Thanks."

Since Special Agent Rickard had been assigned to the task force, Steed had thought there was something about him that just didn't seem right. He didn't fit in with the other officers. After twenty-eight years on the job, officers got a gut feeling about people. Rickard was a man who didn't believe in the team approach that was so crucial in police work.

Steed would keep an eye on him. He had a vested interest. His goddaughter was involved.

CHAPTER 12

DALILAH ENJOYED THE beautiful day in late February. It was unseasonably warm, even for North Carolina, with temperatures in the mid-seventies and not a cloud in the sky. Dalilah listened to her favorite beach music by Chairmen of the Board for the trip down to Morehead City. She was anxious to see Brad again. He seemed the type of man who could love a woman like herself. However, he was into his job, national security and all that macho bullshit. Tonight she would forget all that and enjoy a nice hunk of American beefcake. But she wouldn't forget she was there on business.

Her mind wandered back to the brief and intel reports. How could anyone use someone else's body to transport diamonds, and who knows what else? What happened to the sanctity of death, burial, family, church and heaven?

Did war do these things to people? Her dad had often told her that war didn't cause people to behave like animals. Plain greed, power and money caused humans to do things that were totally unimaginable. War just gave them an excuse—and often a little bit of camouflage—to act out their inhumane deeds.

But who came up with the idea of selling Balkan bodies to medical schools? Surely the schools know where these bodies come from, or do they care?

The report stated the cadavers were filled with old Soviet diamonds and shipped to various ports throughout the world. The client in this case wanted to know where in the United States the cadavers were being shipped, who picked them up in port and how they cleared customs so quickly. Brad could help her understand port security, customs and how cargo was transferred from the large ships to port storage.

Dalilah was getting close to Brad's house. He lived just one block from U.S. Highway 70, the main highway from Raleigh to Morehead City. Dalilah slowed down and checked her makeup in the rear view mirror. As she pulled into the driveway, she saw him waiting at the door.

***

Another car out of Dalilah's sight had also just arrived in Morehead City. The male Caucasian driver lit a cigarette, placed a call on his cell phone and waited to give an update to his supervisor.

CHAPTER 13

THE MIDDLE-AGED MAN donned his captain's hat and, after checking the fuel gauge, told the anxious young sailor to release the bowline. The three-hundred-thousand-dollar yacht, named *Gem of the Sea*, pulled away from the dock and moved slowly through the Intracoastal Waterway toward the Atlantic. It was a beautiful evening, and the sun was just setting. The captain had made this particular run several times in the past year . . . five, to be exact. The destination was almost the same each time, at least three miles off the Carolina coast. He traveled this route only during the evening hours and with only one shipmate. It was easy work, so there was no need for extra hands and eyes.

He brought the yacht to a halt as soon as they reached the imaginary perimeter of international waters. The night came alive with another starry display, and the sky was so clear, the Milky Way shone across the black velvet sky. The captain reached for his binoculars and searched off the starboard bow for three quick flashes of white light. When his eyes found the signal, he engaged the engines and proceeded at fifteen knots toward the beacon. When the boat was within a quarter-mile of the large cargo ship headed for Morehead City, the captain brought the vessel to a drifting stop.

The large transatlantic ship, arriving from northern Europe, was due at the Morehead City port by 2100 hours. Because of new U.S. Coast Guard regulations, tankers and freighters had to provide a seventy-two-hour arrival notice prior to reaching any U.S. port. The Coast Guard and port authorities would then set up boarding inspections to check for dangerous cargo. The Nikolai IV continued on course as four Lithuanian sailors tossed two crates over the stern railing. The containers had flotation devices attached around each side. With calm seas, the crates would be easy to handle.

After the ship had moved away, the captain maneuvered the yacht within gaffing distance of the containers. As the captain watched the large cargo ship reduce its speed near the port, he wondered if the sailors knew any details about the drop.

He turned his attention to his assistant, who now had both crates at the rear landing. The sides of the crates had markings from many different languages. The first mate shouted and pointed to some words in English:

KEEP FROZEN-MEDICAL SUPPLIES.

The captain smiled and looked at the stars twinkling like diamonds in the sky.

CHAPTER 14

THE EVENING WAS going fabulously for Brad and Dalilah. Brad was a Cancer, which made him very domestic. His tidiness and how he cared for his home were not skills he learned in the Marine Corps. Cancers were by nature domestically oriented, and the men were usually great cooks. Brad certainly excelled in this area. He had already chopped all the ingredients for dinner and had set out a tray of spices and sauces to be added at the right moment. He looked like a Chef Warrior, primed for battle with weapons at the ready.

Dalilah headed for the shower to tidy up. She loved a steamy shower and bath. She really enjoyed the water and the energizing effect it had on her. After a wonderful twenty-minute meditation, Dalilah emerged from her watery haven, refreshed and relaxed.

She defogged the mirror with her blow dryer and brushed through her hair. She decided to leave it down for the evening. She checked her face in the mirror, but due to her skin tone and facial features, Dalilah didn't spend a lot of time on cosmetics. She went into the other room to find the perfect outfit. Dalilah emerged from the bedroom dressed to kill in a red silk, form-fitting minidress.

Brad looked up as she came into the kitchen. He captured his composure and softly said, "You look great! My God, you're a goddess!"

Dalilah gave him an approving smile. She enjoyed sincere compliments from her friends, especially her male friends.

Dinner was served on the balcony overlooking the Intracoastal Waterway. A nice breeze off the water brought with it the freshness of the sea. Both Brad and Dalilah looked up at the stars.

"Would you like some more wine?" Brad asked.

"No, thank you," Dalilah replied. She was not a big wine drinker. Her martial arts training demanded discipline, and she didn't like anything that might compromise her senses. Brad was not a big drinker either, just a glass or two with dinner.

"How is your knee?" Dalilah asked. "Is it giving you any trouble?"

"No, not since you fixed it for me."

Dalilah remembered the first time they had met. She had been on the beach at Emerald Isle on the Crystal Coast of North Carolina. It was a perfect day, temperature in the mid-eighties with a slight breeze from the ocean and magical sounds of the surf.

While reading a mystery novel, she had seen Brad wearing headphones and running on the beach. Another man was playing Frisbee with his dog. The dog was on a collision course. In seconds, Brad and the dog were tumbling in the sand. Brad's leg was twisted, causing severe pain in his right knee.

The dog's owner had said, "I'm sorry, man. I didn't mean for my dog to run into you."

Brad just shook his head.

Dalilah knelt beside him and asked, "May I help you? I know a little about energy healing."

Brad, an eight-year veteran of the Marine Corps, heard what she said, but it didn't matter. She was a knockout.

"Sure, anything you can do."

Dalilah spent a few seconds getting relaxed, and then she took three deep breaths. She began by saying, "Cho Ku Rei, Cho Ku Rei, Cho Ku Rei." She also moved her hands in a spiral, making small counterclockwise circles in the air over the injured area. Then she placed her hands on Brad's knee.

Brad felt immense warmth and wondered if she had some type of heat cream on her hands. She didn't. "What exactly are you doing?" he asked.

"It's called Reiki. It means universal energy. It's a form of energy healing that has its roots in Tibetan Buddhism. A Japanese woman brought it to the United States by way of Hawaii. Cho Ku Rei is the Reiki power symbol, and it increases the Reiki energy for healing."

Brad, being a hard-core United States Marine Corps captain and military police officer, thought this was a load of horseshit and New Age, dope-smoking, pseudo-Hollywood philosophy. Yet, he felt the heat, and there was a slight bluish glow around Dalilah's hands. At any rate his knee was better, and he had the attention of the prettiest girl on the beach. He'd keep an open mind.

When Dalilah looked closely into Brad's eyes, she saw them twinkle. Not just a regular twinkle, but a strong, beacon-like flash. She remembered her dad discussing having seen this sunburst glow when he met Dalilah's "bonus mom," his second wife and true soul mate. Dad had said that when soul mates or people from a soul group meet, they see a shining flicker in each other's eyes. A signal from the soul.

That day, Dalilah had seen her first sunburst. She had thought Brad was the one. But after a year or so, they were still just good friends, and not really can't-live-without-you soul mates. Either way, she enjoyed his company, and they had a good time together.

Both Brad and Dalilah laughed whenever they revisited their fateful meeting. Brad confessed he'd really thought she was crazy with all that Reiki stuff. Eventually though, he had not only become a believer, but also a practitioner. Dalilah was a Usui Reiki Ryoho Master and had taught him. She herself had learned the energy healing skill from her father and bonus mom, both Reiki Masters and Teachers.

Reiki Masters teach the Reiki skills and give the energy attunements in ceremonies that allow the student to receive the Reiki energy. This teaching dates back to a Japanese man, Mikao Usui, who rediscovered the ancient healing secrets in the late 1800s. Usui Reiki Ryoho means Usui's method of natural healing.

Once in the United States, it grew popular. Many people wanted to learn the ancient healing secrets of laying-on-of-hands, similar to the tradition found in Christian teachings.

Brad was not a Reiki Master yet. As a level-two practitioner, he had access to the three Reiki symbols: Cho Ku Rei to increase power, Sei Hei Ki for mental/emotional healing, and Hon Sha Ze Sho Nen for sending the Reiki energy anywhere for a distant healing.

Dalilah mentioned to Brad that he might want to learn the Reiki Master level of healing. She moved closer as they snuggled together. Dalilah had to look up to see Brad's twinkling eyes atop his six-foot Nordic frame. He touched her cheek and kissed her. She felt something against her lower body as he pressed closer. Dalilah thought, God, I love my life!

CHAPTER 15

HE CAPTAIN HANDED the pry bar to Ben, his son and assistant. A rite of passage. The operation was too risky to include anyone other than family. He knew his wife had her suspicions, but she was never overbearing about the nightly excursions. The trips happened only about every two months, but the captain was aware of her protective feelings now that their son was involved.

The first crate was loaded onto the rear landing; the captain watched Ben tie it off. He could tell his son was very excited to have an active role in the family business. This was Ben's first trip; and even though it hadn't been discussed, this was a rite of passage.

Father and son pried open the first container. The gelatinous formaldehyde had an eerie, opaque, greenish color. It was cold to the touch. Because of the semi-solid preservative, the crate was quite heavy. Ben held on tight to keep it on the landing platform.

Few customs officers would dare to put their arms and hands into the mixture to search a medical cadaver. This made a perfect delivery system to ship anything, including drugs, anywhere—even to the United States. The gel, being completely nonporous, made a very efficient medium to mask odors. Drug-sniffing dogs never alerted on contraband. This deception had been used many times, and the smugglers had yet to be discovered.

Ben stuck his hand into the cadaver gelatin as directed by his father. He threw large chunks of the sealant into the ocean. He grimaced as he searched for and located the target stitches on the cadaver's sternum. He pulled the stitches apart, and the chest and abdominal cavities opened.

Ben reached inside with one hand. No heart. No lungs. No organs. Unable to get a good grip, he plunged in his second hand and his nose rubbed against the death gel. The stench hit him full force. The smell was horribly concentrated after having been enclosed in a refrigerated container for the transatlantic trip. The odor was too much for him, and he began to heave. Overcome by the foulness, he leaned off the starboard side and spent half an hour donating his dinner to the fishes. Ben's father knew he would be all right.

The captain offered him some wine to freshen his mouth. Looking apologetic, Ben drank it. His father touched his shoulder to reassure him. After two glasses, Ben went back to the first cadaver with renewed appreciation for the family business.

He searched inside the body cavity for the smoothness of a plastic bag. He grabbed it and pulled it upward through the green ooze, throwing it onto the deck.

The captain came alive proudly, "Good job, son. Only four more."

Ben retrieved a total of five two-gallon plastic bags, each weighing five pounds.

Inside each bag were brown, crusty lumps. At least, it looked that way to anyone who didn't know the secret.

Ben focused again on crate number one as his dad told him to search the body cavity again, because sometimes the Russians miscounted. On more than one occasion, extra bags had been found. After a thorough search, Ben cut loose the flotation foam and pushed the crate off the landing.

Down to the bottom of the sea went the crate, formaldehyde and cadaver. Devoid of air-containing organs, the body would not surface. The fish and other marine life would soon dispose of the body; the crate would gently sink and break into pieces flowing north in the warm Gulf Stream current. It was fool proof.

If anyone ever did discover a body or a crate, a logical explanation was ready. The gel had leaked during shipping, and the cadaver had been exposed to air. By the time it reached port, it would be too decayed for research. It had simply been thrown overboard in international waters.

Burial at sea. End of explanation.

The captain watched with pride as Ben finished his job on the second crate. He had removed five more plastic bags. It was a good night—father and son on the open sea working together in the family business. One small jewelry store ten years ago had expanded to ten stores in the USA and one in Europe. Ben's future was set.

CHAPTER 16

DALILAH LED BRAD into the living room as their passion grew. She had a feeling that somehow Brad was different and that he had changed. As a rising Scorpio, her inner self felt a deep longing for him, giving kudos to her psychic, sensual and sexual nature. She could feel the fire in her navel chakra.

She noticed that Brad seemed to be feeling something new, and she hoped it was the same sense of connection and longing. Dalilah knew that Cancers were heavily invested in their emotions and that sometimes the Crab could hold back to hide insecurities. But she could see he was ready to be totally open and vulnerable with her. She knew he trusted her, and she liked it a lot!

Dalilah moved to the sofa as their kisses deepened and their tongues met with frequent and sensual strokes. Moans and groans came from them both. Brad slowly removed the spaghetti strap from her shoulder. Her left breast was exposed, but not for long. Dalilah felt Brad's strong hand cupping her flesh as the floral print was replaced by his gentle touch.

Even though Dalilah was petite, her bosom was pert and full. Brad's lips soon moved to her breast. She arched her back, giving permission for him to indulge his passion on her willing body. Dalilah's hand made its way to his inner thigh where she stroked his boldness.

Brad picked her up and carried her to the bedroom. Once on the bed, he removed her stiletto heels and caressed her lower legs. Dalilah felt him kissing her knee while he gently placed his hand on the outside of her golden-brown thigh. With his other hand, he touched her opposite hip and slowly relieved her of her light blue, French lace panties.

Dalilah looked at Brad as he paused to admire her body.

"You are absolutely beautiful. My own Dalilah goddess!" Brad said in a broken breath.

Dalilah sat up on the edge of the bed as Brad stood in front of her. She unbuttoned his blue tropical-print shirt to rub his firm chest and abdomen. She unbuckled his belt and slowly opened his zipper. His pants succumbed to gravity and landed on the floor. Dalilah admired his gorgeous body. She removed his last piece of clothing and moved in closer. Brad felt her tongue, and his knees began to shake.

Dalilah took her time. She knew how to please someone she loved. She brought him to the brink of ecstasy, then pulled him forward onto the bed. Dalilah turned him over and before he knew it, she was on top. Brad slowly lifted Dalilah's dress over her head. The silky material slipped away and puddled silently on the floor.

Dalilah moved her hips with exotic precision to keep Brad from entering her. The heat was building as she slid back and forth. Looking deep into Brad's eyes, Dalilah found a twinkling sunburst as she peered into the inner realms of his psyche. She hoped Brad saw her soul beacon beaming back at him. Her heart was shouting with a love that she had never known—soul-level passion, pure and simple.

Dalilah placed her lips close to Brad's mouth as she hovered, feeling his breath and enjoying the spirit of his energy. She was a lioness placing its mouth over the nose of its prey to capture the fleeting spirit. This was the real energy exchange, an exchange of the soul.

Then as if by cosmic cue, they kissed deeply as Dalilah shifted her hips and allowed Brad to enter her moistness. It was a coming together of lips, a coming together of souls.

Dalilah felt the Kundalini energy as it flashed up her spine, and the exhilaration propelled her Spirit into the ethers, spiraling higher and higher. She knew Brad had experienced the same feeling as he released his love deep inside her. She marinated in the oneness of the connection as she fully experienced being intertwined in coitus espiritus. Her body was basking with an inner delight and wholeness as she lay on Brad's chest.

The room was filled with a radiating glow of their spiritual union.

Dalilah gazed into Brad's approving eyes. She moved slightly upward so her heart lay on top of his. She felt his strong heartbeat. Her heart synchronized with his. They were one.

CHAPTER 17

SPECIAL AGENT RICKARD opened the phone book to the yellow pages, a basic staple for any investigator. He was searching for the largest jewelry stores in the Central Triad region, especially businesses that were franchises. He found four possible leads and jotted down their names, addresses and phone numbers. He planned to visit each of these stores today to get a feel for their business practices and inventory controls.

***

Sergeant Steed walked past Rickard's cubicle and gave him a courteous nod. Steed still did not care for his behavior. He couldn't put his finger on it, but in time he would find out what he needed to know. Steed went to his desk and called EarthStar International. He was hoping Dalilah had checked in and could brief him on some details of her case.

Liza answered the phone in her usual courteous and professional manner. "EarthStar International, how may I help you?"

"Liza, this is Kyle. How are you?"

"Oh, I'm just peachy, honey. How about you?"

"I'm doing just fine. I'm calling to see if Dalilah has checked in."

Liza responded in her sultry voice, "Yes, Kyle. She's in Morehead City now with Brad of the Marine Patrol."

"Any more tails?"

"Not that she said."

"Well, okay, then. Just thought I'd check. You know, we ought to do lunch soon and get caught up on things."

"Yes, that would be wonderful, Kyle."

Kyle had known Liza for several years, especially since she had been the secretary for CID. Their relationship was friendly, and they often went to lunch together.

Kyle was hesitant in his approach to anything resembling a romantic interest. Liza was the only woman he talked to in a cordial manner. He was part of the divorce statistic so typical in the police profession. His marriage had been dissolved for over ten years. Eighty percent of all male police officers were divorced, along with ninety-nine percent of all female officers.

Kyle knew all about Liza's fifteen-year marriage to a police officer and her divorce. He assumed it was the same situation, not exactly anybody's fault. People just grew apart.

He was still lamenting his own divorce and wasn't ready for a long-term relationship. As a matter of fact, he didn't know what he was ready for. He rarely thought about it. His divorce had taken a heavy toll on his psyche. He had thought everything was fine in his marriage. Then one day his wife told him she'd had enough and wanted a divorce. Kyle was floored. Their sexual life had been zilch, and he knew his wife was unhappy about his lack of intimacy. He had become complacent in life, especially with his sexual drive. All he wanted to do was retire in two years, go fishing and let the world go by. His ex-wife had other plans. Kyle knew she wanted excitement, travel and to live in exotic places. He could not accommodate her.

Working as a police officer had taken Kyle's spirit. He was a walking zombie. He did not care for his job, the court system, the promotions made within the department or for anything. His soul was null and void. Somewhere along the line, he had become dull. The only spark in Kyle's life was Liza.

CHAPTER 18

SIZZLING BACON AND the grinding of fresh coffee awakened Dalilah. She went to the bathroom to freshen up. A little water in her dark hair, some moisturizer on her face, and she looked like a model on a photo shoot.

In the kitchen Brad had already chopped onions, green peppers, ham and cheese to make scrambled omelettes. Dalilah had made this special dish the last time they had been together, along with cheesy grits. She had learned the secret to scrambled omelettes—cooking all the ingredients first, then adding the eggs—from her dad, who fixed them for her every time she went home for an overnight visit.

Dalilah put the eggs on a platter and took them to the balcony where Brad had set the table. She looked into his eyes and smiled. It was a bright, sunny day.

Before finishing breakfast, Dalilah asked if Brad could take her a few places for information on container ships, shipping manifests, customs declarations and cargo storage. She was careful not to tell him specifically what she was looking for. She planned to visit North Carolina's two main ports, Morehead City and Wilmington. Morehead City was the logical first choice since Brad lived there.

Brad asked, "Is there anything special you're looking for?"

"I'm looking for medical cadavers," she said with a straightforward look. "A client has requested information about any biological threats from the bodies coming from countries on the State Department's quarantine list. The concern is that students might be contaminated if a virus like MRSA were attached to a cadaver, so I'm looking for improper shipping, packing and refrigeration that might create a breeding ground. One of the state legislators has a son in medical school, and he doesn't want him to be a victim. This is a preliminary investigation to find the protocol for medical cadavers."

Dalilah had given Brad enough information to satisfy his investigative curiosity. She liked talking about her case to him, but he didn't need to know everything. She decided to play it by ear and allow the day to develop. Dalilah knew Brad well enough to know that he would do anything to help her.

Brad cleaned up the kitchen as Dalilah headed for the shower. He changed into a blue buttoned-down oxford with khaki pants, his casual duty attire. He had a pair of coveralls in the SUV if he had to do any messy police work.

Dalilah was on the job now, and she needed information. Most of it would come from men, so she had to capture their attention right away. She wore a white cotton blouse unbuttoned at the neck with a mid-thigh-length khaki skirt. Men really were easy.

They left in Brad's official Marine Patrol Chevrolet TrailBlazer and headed for the harbormaster's main office. Dalilah didn't waste any time. She was in investigative mode, and she worked like a machine. "Which warehouses do they keep the cadavers in—how often so the Russian freighters come in—do you personally inspect each cargo?" Touching his arm and shoulder frequently and standing close, she rattled off questions and follow-ups so fast the harbormaster could hardly catch his breath.

Brad had known John for about three years. John was a good ol' Southern boy. He immediately took a liking to Dalilah, and she knew it. She finally got to the real point of her inquiries. She asked about refrigerated cargo, where it would be unloaded and where it would be inspected. The refrigerated warehouse was located off Pier 18 on Port Terminal Road. Dalilah finished her questions, then reached up to give John a hug. John blushed from ear to ear and told her to come back anytime if she needed any more help. He winked at Brad as they both left.

"How far is Pier 18 from here?" Dalilah asked.

"About half a mile," Brad said, "so we'll be there in five minutes."

As they were leaving the parking lot, Brad's radio came alive. "Unit Sierra Two Five, 10-20?" Sierra was the designation for the sergeant on duty.

Brad picked up the microphone and responded, "Unit Sierra Two Five, Harbor Master's office."

"10-4, Unit Sierra Two Five, 10-17 at the Holiday Inn in Atlantic Beach for a large bag of medical waste that washed up with this morning's tide."

"10-4, ETA 20 minutes."

Dalilah knew her police ten-codes, so she knew Brad had to go see the complainant about the medical waste. Since the call required that he head in the opposite direction, he dropped Dalilah off at her car.

"I'll catch up with you in about an hour at Pier 18," he said.

"Great! That will be fine."

After receiving directions from Brad, Dalilah got into her red Sebring and headed to Port Terminal Road. Her thoughts were energized with the new information as she got deeper into the case. Now she had a physical location of the cadavers; she needed a plan to access the warehouses without authorization.

***

A dark sedan headed in the same direction. The driver pulled out his cell phone and made a brief call. "We're on the move. She's by herself. I'll contact you later."

CHAPTER 19

IT WAS MONDAY morning, and Ben's father, Joseph, waited patiently while his son gathered his books. He had driven Ben to school since the third grade. The ritual started because of bullying on the school bus and had continued even into his senior year.

Joseph believed in a public school, secular education for his son. After all, when Ben graduated from college, those kids who were his classmates would be his customers. Ben would have to know how to speak to them, and more importantly, how to sell to them. Joseph was always thinking business, and he wanted to pass this lesson on to his son. It was a trait he had learned from his own father, a silver merchant.

As he dropped him off in front of the office, Joseph reminded his son, "Ben, we have business to finish today after school."

"I remember, Papa."

Joseph knew Ben wanted to be an athlete and play sports like the other kids. "Papa, this is my senior year. I'd really like to be on the swim team!"

But Joseph had planned Ben's life, and sports were not part of the package. The noticeable frustration Ben expressed at times was taken in stride, as Joseph understood his son did not yet know the full nature of the family empire. Ben was an exceptional swimmer, but swimming would not pay the bills nor help him manage the business.

Since the jewelry store was closed on Mondays, Joseph made rounds to catch up with business associates. They were often the same people . . . bankers, stockbrokers and, most importantly, his accountant. Not just any accountant, but his own younger brother, Hiram Davidson. Joseph believed in trusting only family with business ventures, especially high-risk entrepreneurship.

Hiram was the only other soul, locally, who knew the entire picture of Joseph's business dealings, holdings, properties and investments. Not even Joseph's wife or son knew the extent of his enterprises.

The afternoon quickly approached, and Joseph made his way back to the school. Ben was waiting at the front entrance for his father's Mercedes. Most of the youth's friends had already driven away in their own cars, but Joseph was admittedly overprotective because of the risky nature of his business. Father and son engaged in small talk about their day. It did not take long to arrive at Ben's Fine Jewelry Emporium in Morehead City.

The business was decorated in a desert oasis motif. An impressive six-foot fountain greeted customers at the front door, along with a well-mannered host to help each patron with his or her special needs. Plates of cheese, fruit and wine were elegantly displayed. There were sitting areas for couples as they made their final decisions. Joseph spared no expense for the atmosphere of ultimate customer service. Armed security guards—or safety officers as Joseph called them—were always present, yet very discreet.

Joseph interviewed each of the safety officers personally. He did not trust the average security company to provide professionalism on a contract basis. The man in charge of security for his entire business was an old Army friend, a former intelligence officer for the Israeli Army. Joseph hired only the best to protect his business and family. He had never been robbed. A rumor circulated among the employees that Joseph was a retired agent with Mossad, Israel's CIA. He never told anybody anything to the contrary.

Ben grabbed two brown paper bags from the car and followed his father into the back workroom where, on days when the store was open, three craftsmen performed jewelry repair and design. He placed the bags on a table and went back to the car to retrieve two more. To the casual observer, he was just carrying in groceries for the staff kitchen, a task he did almost every Monday afternoon.

Joseph turned on the ultrasonic jewelry cleaner, a large metal container about the size of a shoebox filled with cleaning chemicals. Since this was Ben's first experience in this part of the business, Joseph explained the exact procedure for him to follow. Ben unloaded the grocery bags, which contained the plastic bags retrieved from the cadavers. Joseph opened one and dumped the lumpy brown mixture into the ultrasonic cleaner. The chemical bath had no problems removing the crusty layers.

The diamonds had been coated with liquefied oatmeal as camouflage. The plastic bags looked as if they were filled with dirt or spoiled food. Either way, if the bags were discovered or left out, nobody would give them a second glance. They would probably be thrown in the trash. And if one of the diamonds fell out, nobody would suspect it to be a valuable gemstone. Most people fail to recognize the brilliance within when looking at a diamond in the rough with its brown, earthy and crusted exterior.

After three minutes, Joseph removed the strainer and dumped the contents onto a black velvet cloth. The metamorphosis was complete. The stones glittered like miniature stars. Over ten thousand carats of pure Russian lab-created diamonds lay on the table.

"Ben, it's your turn."

Joseph watched his son work with a comfortable purpose and steadfastness, as he efficiently emptied another bag of crusty diamonds into the cleaner.

Ben was a quick study, and Joseph was very proud of him. The boy would be an important man one day in his community. Joseph would make sure of that.

Both father and son looked at the glistening table as they surveyed the treasures. Joseph had been teaching Ben about the jewelry business and gemstones since his son was in second grade. Ben was quite taken with the scientific part of the business.

"Son, a carat is two hundred milligrams, and a five-pound bag contains a little more than ten thousand carats. We sell diamonds at the wholesale rate between three to five hundred dollars per carat, depending on the quality of the stone. For long-time business associates, the price is one hundred dollars per carat," explained Joseph. He saw the excitement in Ben's eyes.

"No wonder, Papa, you're the most popular diamond distributor on the East Coast!"

Joseph continued with the specifics of the diamond trade. "One five-pound bag of Russian diamonds at wholesale brings in a minimum cool million. When we sell the diamonds in any of our retail stores, either in mounted jewelry or as loose diamonds, we can charge seven hundred to one thousand dollars per carat. You do the math. And our retail price is still well below any of our competitors."

Joseph had a special arrangement with his Russian partners. His price for ten bags, ten thousand carats each, with shipping and handling, was one hundred thousand dollars US. The minimum potential profit was a modest ten million.

Joseph looked at his son. "Ben, you will be a wealthy man for the rest of your life."

Ben was speechless. Both father and son gazed at the table as Ben lightly touched the gems. Diamonds of every size and cut sparkled as Ben's eyes glazed over, and he whispered, "Ten million dollars."

Joseph was glad he had involved Ben in the operational aspects of the business. At almost eighteen, Ben had most of the picture. At least he had what he needed for now. Joseph didn't want to tell him everything. He wanted Ben to learn slowly and on a need-to-know basis.

Joseph continued to give more information for Ben to absorb. "The deliveries are made by ocean freighter every three or four months. There is no reason to believe this should stop any time in the near future. But we can always get out if we need to. Our retirement fund can sustain us through two generations. Son, I have worked hard my whole life and now, I want you to benefit from my struggles."

Ben smiled. "Thanks, Papa."

His son had one plan—get a degree in business, which would take only three years with Joseph's resources. It helped that he was on the board of directors at the local university. The degree would simply be window-dressing for an already lucrative and established career. Joseph wanted his son to be even more successful than he.

Joseph was not a greedy man, despite the façade, and he was careful in his selection of diamonds he marketed. Diamonds over two carats would be heavily inspected and possibly detected as being lab-created. However, diamonds in the one-carat, half-carat and even quarter-carat range would hardly be subjected to such scrutiny.

Half-carat and quarter-carat diamonds would be used in multiple settings for various types of jewelry. Tennis bracelets, earrings and pendants would host several smaller diamonds to create a beautiful piece.

He would use several diamonds to make solitaires in the range of half-carat to full-carat rings. Nobody would suspect these diamonds were lab-created, especially since they came from a reputable dealer. Joseph was also careful in buying only white diamonds, since colored diamonds met with multiple layers of inspection. Joseph wanted to be beyond suspicion.

Greedy jewelers might opt for the larger Russian diamonds of two to four carats, hoping for sales in excess of $50,000. The larger diamonds would no doubt go to De Beers for verification and authenticity. De Beers, the world's largest diamond dealer, had the equipment to determine if the gemstones were man-made. The greedy jewelers always got caught. Joseph had never once been accused of selling lab-created diamonds. He was careful about where and to whom he sold. Even though some of his business associates suspected something, they never balked at Joseph's offerings because, in the end, they also made huge profits.

Ben had arranged the diamonds by carats per Joseph's instructions and placed them in separate containers. Before the end of the day, the diamonds would be transferred to the in-store vault, to which only Joseph had access. Joseph would then make the necessary calls to alert the wholesale buyers about the recent shipment.

After securing the vault and setting the store alarm, Joseph and Ben went home. It had been another good day as father and son worked together to build a financial empire and a legacy for many generations.

Arriving home, Joseph kissed his wife, Sarah, as she continued to set the table for dinner. They had invited friends for a Hawaiian luau with lots of fruits, salads and fish. After the main course, Sarah brought out the dessert tray. It was a beautiful tropical display of whipped cream, cherries, pineapple and coconut—all on a bed of lime-green JELL-O. Joseph looked at Ben and grinned, knowing he would be thinking of the cadaver crates.

Joseph stood as he served the dessert. "Eat up, my son. Your mother has worked very hard preparing this beautiful meal."

CHAPTER 20

DALILAH MADE HER way down Port Terminal Road and immediately found Pier 18, where the refrigerated warehouse was located. It was exactly as Brad had said. She knew he would be with her shortly, always a good back-up partner. Dalilah parked and immediately looked for her flashlight, a Maglite, the kind used by police officers worldwide. Constructed of tubular aircraft aluminum with three D-size batteries, it was a dangerous weapon, especially in Dalilah's hands.

She needed only one more thing as she looked in her canvas bag in the back seat, a bright red NCSU windbreaker she won in a sorority fundraiser. She wasn't sure how long she would be inside; and since the warehouse was refrigerated, she thought she'd better be prepared.

At the guard shack a radio was playing, but she didn't see any security guards. Maybe they were on break or making their rounds. Odd that they left their post unattended. Dalilah found the main entrance right away. By the looks of the place, it had been here for some time, probably since before she was born. She pushed on the rusted steel door. Again her intuitive side sounded an alarm, but her logical side did an override. She entered the building.

As she moved through the entrance, she gripped her flashlight firmly. The warehouse was dark and a bit eerie. It was chilly inside, so she put on her jacket.

The warehouse was poorly lighted, so she began looking for light switches. None were by the door, but she found an old circuit-breaker box. Dalilah checked all the breakers, and they were all working, so dim light it would be.

She turned on her Maglite and searched for the wooden crates that contained the cadavers. She wasn't sure they were in this particular warehouse, but this was where the harbormaster had said to look. As she searched each section, she found only produce from South America awaiting USDA inspection and customs clearance.

Dalilah made her way to the far end of the space and found a smaller room with the lights on. She opened the door and said loudly, "Hello, is anybody in here?"

There was no answer, so Dalilah snooped for anything that might give her a clue. As she rounded a corner of boxes stacked about eight feet high, she saw some wooden crates. They were labeled with many languages—French, Spanish, Greek, Japanese, Russian and English. Then she saw what she was looking for—crates with the words, KEEP FROZEN—MEDICAL SUPPLIES.

She found about a hundred wooden boxes stacked five high on wooden pallets. Dalilah looked around for a pry bar, but she found only a rusted metal bar lying on the floor. *This will do.* She searched for a path to the top of the crates.

She crawled onto some adjacent boxes and jumped across to the cadaver crates. Inserting the metal bar beneath the top wooden layer, she jerked upward. The top moved a little, so she pried up the other nails securing the lid. Soon she could lift the lid.

Dalilah shined her flashlight into the container and saw green gelatin with a body floating inside. It looked surreal, like a horror movie. She was surprised that there was no odor of decaying flesh. The green sealant really did suppress the body odors, but not the stench of the formaldehyde.

She recalled the case intel in her mind. Supposedly, the internal organs were removed from the chest and abdominal cavities and replaced with diamonds. Reluctantly, Dalilah rolled up her jacket sleeves and put her left hand inside the cadaver gel. She scooped enough formaldehyde away to expose the chest. She searched the right side of her belt and removed a serrated 440 stainless steel folding knife. It easily cut through the sutures at the sternum. As she pulled the chest cavity open, the putrid stench hit her head-on. She lurched backward and almost heaved. Regaining her balance on top of the crates, she leaned away and took some deep breaths. Dalilah had not thought of bringing some Vicks VapoRub to place under her nostrils to mask the smell.

With a persistent attitude, she went back to the cadaver and looked inside the chest cavity. The only things she saw were body parts. Real body parts. She knew that she couldn't possibly search every crate. There had to be a better way. She closed the chest cavity and pushed the gel on top of the cadaver.

As she replaced the lid, she heard a noise and froze. It sounded as if a steel pipe had fallen to the floor. She decided not to call out as she scurried down the side of the crates. Her adrenaline was pumping, so she hardly noticed the thirty-eight degree temperature inside the warehouse.

Dalilah found a spot between some boxes and put her back against the wall so that no one could surprise her from behind. She remembered her tactical training about building searches, cover and concealment.

She waited about five minutes and heard nothing but rats making their way through the produce. Maybe it was just a false alarm and an overactive imagination. After all, the building was really old, and something may have just fallen off the walls or from the ceiling.

Dalilah decided to go back outside to locate the guards. Just to be on the safe side, she walked slowly on her tiptoes, ready for anything. When she rounded some large containers, someone grabbed her left arm and yelled, "Gotcha!"

Wheeling around, Dalilah raised her Maglite to a ready position and illuminated the dark figure. In a split second, she concentrated her chi by sounding a loud "No!" and struck downward with lightning speed. The flashlight found its mark, and she heard a loud groan. The Maglite made a direct impact on a pressure point located in the upper forearm called the radial nerve.

With any serious impact to a nerve pressure point, the brain and autonomic nervous system automatically shut down the affected limb. Some pressure points can be affected only by touch, while others must be activated with a strike or kick. Dalilah knew her pressure points, as they were part of the test for her second-degree black sash in Tai Chi.

The assailant's arm had gone limp from the forearm to the fingers . . . all, of course, with severe pain. Dalilah felt the grasp released and heard someone fall. She directed the flashlight beam into his eyes, blinding him.

"Oh, my God! I am so sorry!" she said to the older man wearing a security guard's outfit.

"Okay, okay, just don't hit me again!"

She reached down to help. The older man held his right forearm and said, "I think you broke my arm. What did you hit me with?"

Dalilah immediately put her hand on his forearm to soothe the pain. She activated the Reiki healing energy with a whispered, "Cho Ku Rei, Cho Ku Rei, Cho Ku Rei."

The security guard thought he saw a blue glow surrounding his arm. Then he dismissed the vision, thinking it might have been the low lighting, or the tumble he took. Or maybe he was having a stroke. In minutes his arm was normal again. As a matter of fact, it had never felt better.

He said, "I just came back from a bathroom break and found the front door open, so I thought I'd better check it out. Sometimes kids will play inside the old warehouses around the port."

In the dark, Dalilah had looked like a young girl. He had grabbed her because he was too old to even think about chasing someone.

Dalilah walked with him back outside; and when there was enough light to see her face, he just smiled. "Now how could a pretty little thing like you put a man like me flat on his back? Where did you learn to take care of yourself like that?" he asked.

"My dad is a retired police officer."

"Hey, he taught you well."

Dalilah smiled. "Yes, he did."

"Now tell me, little lady, why you were walking around that cold warehouse. It's thirty-some degrees in there!"

Dalilah told him she was looking for cadavers to inspect them before delivery to the medical schools. She had rehearsed her reply earlier. She always had a story, and she could always tell it convincingly. "I'm doing quality control inspections for the State to make sure the medical cadaver containers are not leaking possible contaminants into the environment. After I inspected the shipping containers, I looked for a delivery manifest. That's when I heard a noise in the warehouse."

"I didn't hear anything. I was just startled when I saw you. Sorry about grabbing your arm. I have an inventory and delivery manifest in the guard shack if you'd like to see it."

They walked back to the main entrance. The guard sifted through several clipboards until he found the delivery and pick-up schedules. The cadavers were due to be picked up mid-week by the University of North Carolina at Chapel Hill School of Medicine and Duke University School of Medicine in Durham. That was all the information he had for now. Dalilah thanked him and again apologized for hitting him.

He moved his arm without pain and said, "Works like new, so I guess I'll live."

Dalilah was so convincing the guard never asked to see any identification. She hugged him before leaving and once again apologized.

She drove out of the lot just as Brad turned the corner.

"Sorry for being so late, Dalilah. Paper work. Anything here?"

"No, dead end. Nice security guard though. What if we head back to your place. I need to wash off."

***

In the back corner of the warehouse, a bright light shattered the darkness as it gave life to a cigarette. The security guard had not discovered the man, nor had Dalilah been aware of his presence. After finishing his smoke, he made his way out the side door and walked about a block to his car. He would check the boyfriend's residence to see if Dalilah had gone there. If not, he would wait. She would be at Brad's sometime, and he was being paid to wait, watch and report. So, he would wait.

CHAPTER 21

DALILAH CAME OUT of the bathroom as the steam filled the hallway. She felt human and clean again. Brad gave her a juicy kiss, and she obligingly returned his advances. She gave him a big squeeze and pulled away. Her mind was full of questions with no answers in sight.

"How was your case?" Dalilah asked.

"Nothing but a bag of stuff. I took it to Carteret General Hospital. They have an incinerator, eighteen-hundred degrees."

"How did it go at the warehouse?" Brad asked.

"I found the cadavers, but there wasn't really anything to it. Just half-frozen bodies in wooden crates surrounded by this green oozing JELL-O. Kind of sci-fi, you know?"

"I didn't realize we shipped cadavers through this port. Makes me wonder what else goes through this place. Who was the security guard? Maybe I know him."

"He had Tom on his name tag. He was a nice man. And how often do you get calls with medical waste?" Dalilah asked with hopes of changing the conversation. She didn't want to explain how she had hit Tom.

"Too often. SSDD." Same Shit, Different Day, as her dad would say.

Brad continued, "Sometimes I think I'm just spinning my wheels here. I need to start seriously looking for another line of work."

Dalilah didn't respond. Brad had once asked about working with her as a partner. Her refusal to allow Brad to be her business partner had been a major blow to their friendship, and it had hurt Brad's ego tremendously. He came to his senses and forgot about it. Dalilah knew he wouldn't deal well with high-society clients. Brad was a straightforward, shoot-from-the-hip and tell-it-like-it-is kind of guy.

Sometimes Dalilah's work required a little finesse and soft shoe. Plus, she really liked working alone. She worked with an intuitive sense, and a partner would have to give her lots of room for her modus operandi. She hated to explain her actions and reasons because some of her actions didn't even make sense to her at the time. However, every time Dalilah followed her intuition, it paid off.

Dalilah wanted to get off this subject. "I know there's more information here about my investigation. I can feel it. Maybe the Coast Guard can help us."

"I've got a Coast Guard buddy at Fort Macon. Maybe he can steer us in the right direction."

"Will they talk to me?"

"Dalilah, they're men. Of course, they'll talk to you. Maybe not what you want to talk about, but they'll talk. Anyway, they could have some useful information. Remember last summer when I told you about the Turkish sailor?"

Dalilah remembered a story about a dead sailor. It was even on the news in Greensboro. "Is that the one who washed up on shore—"

"A Turkish sailor washed up on Bald Head Island near Wilmington, and I assisted the Coast Guard in the investigation. The sailor had fallen off the ship en route to Wilmington. The captain of the ship never notified any American authorities. If the man hadn't washed up, nobody locally would have been the wiser. If he had, we would've taken him to the morgue and tagged him John Doe."

A light bulb went off in Dalilah's head. "If the sailors did not have to be accounted for, then how about the cargo? How does the company know that its freight arrived at port safely and in the same condition as when it was shipped?"

"The manifest on the ship must coincide with the cargo onboard, and the Coast Guard will often do spot inspections to ensure the paperwork agrees with the cargo."

Dalilah was still not satisfied. The whole process seemed very haphazard. "Who follows up to ensure this happens? With an average cruise time of two weeks from Europe to the USA, anything can happen to cargo. And how are the discrepancies handled, and where do the inconsistencies get reported?"

"I imagine that the ship's captain would be ultimately responsible for the cargo just like the captain of the *Exxon Valdez* and the Alaskan oil spill. The captain would probably call the home office. But I doubt the home office, especially if it's in another country, would make any notifications officially."

"Exactly," Dalilah said as her mind was circling. "Who can we ask that would know for sure?"

"The Coast Guard. They're responsible for boarding the ships and conducting inspections. They have the authority to board any ship within the three-mile boundary of the United States for safety inspections. Since 9/11, they've been given a stronger mandate to muster up their inspection capabilities and to monitor all vessels coming into American ports."

"Is there anybody we can talk to about this now?"

"We can go to the Coast Guard station here in Morehead City. My buddy, the lieutenant, is the one in charge of all searches aboard cargo vessels."

Dalilah changed clothes and called Liza to give her a quick update. Then she turned to Brad, "What are we waiting for?"

She was now in business mode. Nothing could stop her.

CHAPTER 22

LIZA WAS APPLYING some last-minute touches of cherry red lipstick. She felt like a schoolgirl going on a first date. Even though she had given birth to one child, Liza kept a slim figure and was quite attractive. She worked out regularly, ate the right foods and took care of her skin. She was a class act and an ever hopeful romantic.

When the door opened, she thought it was Kyle. They had scheduled a lunch date today at the local, uptown Mellow Mushroom, and he was always very punctual. However, a disappointed Liza saw a young Caucasian man with unshaven stubble.

"Welcome to EarthStar International. May I help you?"

The man replied in broken English with a thick Eastern European accent, perhaps Russian. "Yes, I am looking for Miss Smith. Is she in?"

Liza, being very careful about divulging any information, replied, "May I ask who is inquiring?"

The man, in an attempt to be aloof, simply stated, "I am Mr. Jones. I had an appointment with her today to discuss my case."

Liza immediately became suspicious. "And what case would that be? I'm Miss Smith's administrative assistant. If you can give me the case number, perhaps I'll be able to assist you."

"I really don't have the case number. I was told by Miss Smith to meet her here at noon today."

Liza looked at her appointment book. "I don't see an appointment for you, Mr. Jones. Perhaps it was another day."

The man then moved closer to Liza's desk and began to look through some papers. Liza stood and said, "I don't think you should be looking—"

The man pushed her down into her seat. She sat there breathless. Then she reached into her purse, removed a can of aerosol repellent and ignited his face with police-issue pepper spray, a retirement gift from the detective bureau. The pepper spray was ten percent red pepper extract, the same type of canister issued to police officers.

Mr. Jones screamed and groped for Liza as he intermittently clawed at his face. Every time he touched his eyes, the pepper extract burned even worse. She watched as he stumbled around the office, mumbling curse words in some foreign tongue, and finally tripped over the coffee table.

He regained his balance and wiped his face with his coat sleeve. With squinted eyes, he saw a blurred image of Liza through his burning tears. She was still standing by her desk, pepper spray in hand. He made a move, but before he got across the room, he felt a jarring pain the entire length of the right side of his body. Sergeant Kyle Steed had arrived and with his fist hammered the man's suprascapular pressure point—located on top of the shoulder deep inside the trapezius muscle—with his fist.

Mr. Jones lay on the floor with his left arm paralyzed. Steed bent the suspect's arm into a chicken wing and pounced on his writhing body with a knee in his back. After handcuffing the man, Steed did a quick cursory search around the suspect's backside and waist for weapons.

"Are you all right?" he asked Liza.

"I am now," she said in a matter-of-fact tone.

Sergeant Steed grabbed his radio, "Car 901, Signal One, 10-33." The codes indicated he had initiated police action and it was an emergency.

The dispatcher replied, "Car 901."

"Car 901, 10-95 with a 10-69 suspect at EarthStar International in the Jefferson Standard Building, 101 North Elm Street. I need a patrol unit for transport."

"10-4, car 901."

Liza knew the ten-codes meant Kyle had an assault suspect in custody. Since they were only two blocks from the police department, help arrived in less than two minutes. Sergeant McDonald was first on the scene. He kept staring at Liza while Steed explained how she had fought and maced the suspect. "One tough chick," he said.

And she still looked immaculate, hair neat, lipstick unsmudged.

Sergeant Steed said, "Take him to the hospital to have his eyes washed out. After you clear the hospital, I'll meet you in CID and we'll find out what this asshole's problem is."

Another officer arrived to assist Sergeant McDonald. After the suspect was escorted out, Kyle and Liza hugged. She was so thankful Kyle had gotten there a little early. The adrenaline was shutting down, and she felt a little shaken. She trembled slightly. As she leaned against Kyle, Liza thought any woman would be lucky to have him as a partner.

"Did he touch you or harm you in any way?" Kyle asked.

"He pushed me in the chest, and I fell into my chair."

"Are you in any pain or discomfort?"

"No, I'm fine. I still have a little padding up top, so quit making a fuss over me. Let's go eat."

Kyle and Liza walked out after straightening up the office a bit. "Kyle, thank you so very much for coming to my rescue."

"Oh, think nothing of it. It looked as if you had everything under control. I'm just glad you didn't shoot him. We would never have gotten out of there for lunch."

Both of them laughed as they walked together, arms linked.

CHAPTER 23

DALILAH AND BRAD headed north on Highway 58 to the 5th District U.S. Coast Guard Station #151 located at Fort Macon, a North Carolina historic park. Fort Macon was an earthen fortress used during the Civil War to protect the Carolina port from the Northern Navy. It stood in its original location on the east end of Bogue Banks, west of the Beaufort Inlet Channel.

The Fort Macon Coast Guard Station maintained constant vigilance to render aid to distressed mariners, to ensure the working order of navigational markers, to conduct search-and-rescue operations and to enforce federal laws from boating safety to drug interdiction. They were also tasked under the Homeland Security Department to perform cargo and shipping vessel inspections.

It was beneficial to have the Coast Guard Station near Brad's Marine Patrol headquarters since the two organizations worked closely with each other. Each agency often asked for assistance from the other. As a local liaison, Brad also enjoyed riding the big cutters during boarding inspections of cargo ships that had failed to announce their arrival within the established time frames.

Dalilah was sure to be a hit among the Coast Guard men. Brad steered her toward the commandant's office to find the officer on watch. Brad's friend and coworker, Lieutenant Roberts, was on duty. They waited in the office as a chief petty officer announced their arrival.

Dalilah walked around the sterile room and read all the posters, thinking that this place needed a woman's touch. The men watched as she paced and asked her at least ten times if she wanted any coffee, Coke or water. She smiled each time and pleasantly said, "No, thank you."

A particular Coast Guard poster caught her eye. It read,

*The United States Coast Guard
on an average day will:*

◊ *Conduct over 100 missions of search and rescue*

◊ *Save 10 lives and assist over 190 persons in distress*

◊ *Protect over $2,000,000 in property*

◊ *Launch nearly 400 small-boat missions*

◊ *Log over 300 hours in aircraft operations*

◊ *Board approximately 150 vessels*

◊ *Seize almost $10,000,000 in marijuana and cocaine*

◊ *Detain 15 illegal migrants*
◊ *Conduct port safety checks and board 100 large vessels*
◊ *Respond and contain 20 hazardous chemical spills*
◊ *Maintain and service 135 navigational aids*

Dalilah thought to herself that these guys stayed busy. A voice said, "Brad, great to see you. Who's with you?"

"This is Dalilah. She's searching for information on shipping and distribution of products coming from overseas. She's been hired by a business client as sort of an efficiency expert."

Dalilah was thinking that Brad was really getting a handle on giving just the right amount of information so as not to arouse suspicion.

The lieutenant extended his hand. "Jason Roberts. So glad to meet you. I haven't seen you around here."

"I'm Dalilah Smith. I live in Greensboro. I'm just visiting for a couple of days. Brad's showing me around."

"How can I help you?" Lieutenant Roberts asked.

"I've been to the warehouse to inspect some frozen cadavers. I'm interested in knowing how the American ports know exactly what is onboard the large shipping vessels and if there are any changes to cargo, who is notified." She moved closer to the lieutenant. "And how about that Turkish sailor?"

"That was a wake-up call," the lieutenant said. "Up to that moment, there was no requirement for the captain to notify us of missing crewmen or cargo. That has since been changed. So has our mandate to board ships who fail to comply with our 72-hour notification policy."

"But how about the cargo? Could the cargo be dropped off or removed from the ship without notification?"

"Well, it is a big ocean. So, yes, the cargo could be removed, especially in international waters. There really isn't a law that we can enforce for removing cargo on the high seas."

The lieutenant pointed to a map.

"North Carolina alone has over two million acres of sea water to patrol and over four thousand miles of coastline. Along with the Marine Patrol, we also protect and patrol our territorial boundaries of three miles offshore. That doesn't even take into account the federally protected species, some of which must be enforced out to two hundred miles offshore."

Dalilah didn't want to know how to protect oyster beds or contain toxic spills. She needed to know how the diamonds got to their final destination. There had to be another way for the diamonds and the cadavers to be retrieved by someone here on the destination end.

The lieutenant continued staring at Dalilah.

Brad put his arm around her and asked, "Is there anything else, sweetheart?"

Dalilah extended her hand to the lieutenant and said, "That's it for me. Thank you very much for your help. Let me get your name right so I can include it in my report to my client. That's Lieutenant Jason Roberts, right?"

"Yes, it is. Stop by any time, Miss Smith. We are at your service."

"Thank you again," Dalilah said with a beautiful smile as she and Brad left the office.

"Thank you, Brad. At least we tried. At least I know what I'm up against now."

"I hope that helped a little."

"It did."

Brad opened the door for Dalilah. With such a high seat, Dalilah had to step up to get into the TrailBlazer. As she did, a nice brown thigh showed through the slit in her skirt. Dalilah liked it when Brad looked at her, and she let him see just enough.

CHAPTER 24

KYLE AND LIZA enjoyed lunch at the hotel restaurant. The old city fire station had been renovated into a quaint yet upscale eatery and midday hangout for urban professionals. Since they were pressed for time, Kyle and Liza opted for the buffet and salad bar.

Liza was still a bit shaken as they talked about the case. "We have never had trouble like this before," she said, "and I'm a little concerned about Dalilah. I haven't been able to reach her about the assault and the foreign guy."

"Now tell me again—what is this case about?" Kyle asked.

"It's supposed to be about some diamonds shipped in cadavers, but that's all I know. I don't know where they're being shipped from or where they're delivered."

It was highly unusual for criminals to be as bold as the suspect had been. Too much attention would be drawn, and the last thing any criminal organization wanted was focus by the police and press. An all-out daytime assault was a drastic measure unless the young operative was new at the game and not sure how to operate in America.

Kyle promised Liza, "I will get to the bottom of this."

Liza looked deeply into his beaming eyes and placed her hand on top of his. She squeezed his hand and said, "I know you will. You have a real interest in this one. After all, she is your goddaughter."

Kyle gave a light squeeze back, gazed into her loving eyes, and replied, "Yes, I do. But Dalilah isn't the only one I'm worried about. I'll let you know if I find out anything from this guy."

When they got back to the office, Kyle walked up with Liza to make sure she was okay. A patrol officer met them at EarthStar International. Kyle briefed the officer, gave him his cell number and told him he would return after interviewing the suspect.

"I'll be right outside the door if you need anything," the young officer assured Liza.

This type of police protection was normally not available since manpower deficiencies couldn't accommodate such a personal touch. However, Liza was still part of the blue line, and the police department "took care of its own."

Liza, with a thankful look, kissed Kyle on the cheek. "See you soon, and thank you again for everything."

"I'll be back shortly."

Kyle returned to his car and called Sergeant McDonald. "Car 901, 10-20 on Car 105?"

"Car 105, 10-20?" the dispatcher repeated, attempting to locate the officer.

"Car 105. En route to CID."

"10-4. Car 901?"

"Car 901, 10-4. ETA, 5."

The dispatcher repeated the command to Sergeant McDonald, who took the suspect to the police department. Kyle began to formulate strategy for the interview. This questioning, however, would have a different tone. It wouldn't be an interview as usual, but more of an interrogation. This man knew something, and two of the most important women in his life were being affected. He would get the answers he needed.

CHAPTER 25

UNKNOWN TO HIS fellow agents and detectives assigned to the joint task force, Special Agent Rickard was assigned to the DEA, the Drug Enforcement Administration. As far as his coworkers were concerned, he was an investigator under the newly formed Department of Homeland Security.

He used a gruff and distant demeanor. He did not want to solicit any personal interaction for now. This worked well for him. No one questioned his whereabouts or his actions. They assumed that he reported directly to the Director of Homeland Security.

His standing operational directives were to find possible locations for the sales and distribution of the fake diamonds, as he called them. He was tasked with finding the local link to the shipment of Russian diamonds to the United States. Special Agent Rickard was one of several DEA agents assigned to police departments along the entire East Coast trying to solve this mystery.

The National Security Agency had given intelligence data to the DEA about drug-smuggling operations in Eastern European countries in concert with Russian crime families. Telephone conversations had been analyzed for any involvement with legitimate cargo shipments filled with heroin. Since the Afghanistan War in the 1980s and subsequent liberation by American troops, the heroin trade had met with uncertain delivery snafus. Being opportunistic business people, some local warlords had contacted Russian factions for help with their distribution problems.

The Russian scientists-turned-entrepreneurs had used medical cadavers successfully for about five years to smuggle lab-created diamonds into the United States and some European outlets. Word had leaked out to the local crime bosses about this avenue, so the problem with delivery of heroin to American soil was solved. The Russians would take their usual forty-percent business fee, and everyone would be happy and make a profit.

The Afghans had no other choice. The average yearly wage for an Afghan male was only three hundred dollars. A sixty-percent take was more than ample for a comfortable life. The Russians were famous for running a tight organization and for impeccable security standards. Few associates lived long enough to make the same mistake twice, which created an environment of brutal efficiency. The Afghan warlords knew their involvement would never be traced back to them.

Special Agent Rickard left the first store on his list. It was in downtown Greensboro and it was the most prestigious in the city, but it offered nothing that would help in the investigation. His next stop would be The Diamond Palace, a local chain, with a half-page ad in the yellow pages. He was concentrating on the larger jewelry outlets in hopes of finding a proper lead.

If Rickard were able to find the local source for the diamonds, he could follow the trail to the distributor and discover how deliveries were made. This would give his agency a clue as to how the heroin network was set up. He didn't care about the diamonds. He just wanted the drugs. He was a crusader and hopefully, this would snowball into an international effort to eradicate this horribly addictive narcotic.

Of course, a promotion would also be offered should he break the case. He deserved it, and he wanted it. Rickard had done his bench time in all the dust bowls and mud holes of third-world countries. And it wasn't easy playing the hard-nosed federal agent everywhere he went. Sometimes he felt lonely, but he knew he was doing what was right.

He headed for the main counter and flashed his badge and ID card. "Special Agent Rickard, Federal Task Force."

The young sales clerk looked startled. "Yes, sir, how may I help you?"

The Diamond Palace appeared to be a well-run facility. It was bright and clean with professionally dressed employees, one of whom met him at the door with a handshake. Rickard walked to the wall next to the register and inspected the business license. He wrote down the tax and license number. Apparently, the Diamond Palace had been operating for fifteen years. He noticed the display cabinets were filled with a nice assortment of diamond jewelry.

DEA supervisors had hypothesized that locally-owned jewelry stores would be the prime candidates for this venture. The well-known, established diamond stores were probably being supplied with real diamonds from De Beers, the number one diamond distributor in the world. The local family-type operations were more susceptible to the easy money the Russian diamonds could provide.

The manager and owner of the store, Mary Brower, moved toward Rickard. "How may I help you today, sir? Are you looking for something unique for that special loved one in your life?"

Mary worked with her husband Chris in his family's jewelry store in New York City, so she was familiar with selling jewelry to local officials. She found it most beneficial if she offered government discounts to local authorities.

Rickard's strategy was to be very direct and somewhat cold in his responses. "I'm looking for fake diamonds being shipped to local jewelry stores."

Ms. Brower, sensing that Rickard was not interested in buying anything, leaned away from him and stopped smiling.

"Sir, my husband and I have been in business for over fifteen years and we have never sold fake diamonds. You can inspect them yourself."

Special Agent Rickard replied in a Joe Friday tone, "That is exactly what I would like to do since you offered."

Ms. Brower escorted Rickard to the vault area in the back of the store. She was ready to provide a 10x loupe for Rickard to use, but he already had out his own. He had learned over the years to be direct with the civilian populace without any niceties or courteous behavior. If people felt tense and fearful about an official government investigation, most would put up with it and hope for a quick ending.

Rickard searched the trays of loose diamonds. "Who is your diamond supplier, De Beers?"

"No, we have a wholesale supplier locally and in New York."

"Really?" Rickard's interest piqued. "Does your local source have a business in Greensboro?"

"No, he lives in Morehead City."

Rickard acknowledged the gut instinct most detectives had when something felt right. This mundane investigation had gathered momentum. He could taste it.

CHAPTER 26

BRAD DROVE HIS patrol vehicle slowly back to his apartment. Dalilah didn't say much. Being the Gemini, she was mentally multi-tasking by being in deep thought, organizing the information she had so far and strategizing her next move. Brad knew she was not in the frame of mind to carry on a conversation, so he just drove and never said a word. Their relationship was growing, and they seemed to know each other quite well. It was different from just two years ago when both of them said lots of things they wished they hadn't.

As he pulled into the driveway, Brad said, "I can make you a sandwich and a salad if you'd like. I think we have enough leftovers to make a decent meal if you want to take a breather and just soak up some rays on the balcony."

Dalilah, still in major thinking mode, paused and said, "Yes, that would be great. I'm so sorry about being absorbed in this. I'm just trying to figure out how they are moving the . . ."

Dalilah caught herself thinking out loud and about to say too much. It would be best if Brad didn't know any more details. "Yes, let's eat. I'm starving all of a sudden."

Brad went to the kitchen and started his preparations.

"You have to love those Cancer boys," Dalilah said loudly enough for Brad to hear.

Brad put together a mid-afternoon lunch in no time. The salad was already fixed, and he nuked the rest of the food in the microwave. Dalilah fixed the tea and added some extra lemon. Nothing like sipping sweet iced tea with lots of lemon on a beautiful, sunny Carolina day.

After their meal, Dalilah looked at Brad in a way she had not for at least two years. He really did seem different. More mature. More secure. And he had tamed that awful, demanding ego. She could see herself truly loving Brad and having a life with him. Her intuitive self told her they had much more in common now than before. Maybe both of them were maturing and tired of being alone.

Dalilah did not want to settle for being alone at the end of the day. She refused to accept that lifestyle. The cumulative effect of going to an empty bed every night somehow played with the concept of completion, like having an unfinished puzzle or no dessert after a fine main course. She wanted to share the end of the day with a soul mate. Her nights of solitude were now blurred with loneliness. She wanted to be in someone's arms, someone who loved her more than life itself. She longed for that now. Dalilah was a romantic, and she trusted Brad was, too.

The sound of squawking seagulls brought Dalilah's attention back to the task at hand. *Thanks, Dad,* she thought. Do not separate your thoughts and your actions. Let them be the same. Be one with everything, and put all your energies into what you are doing. So much for a romantic interlude. But of course, Dad was right. Business first. Pleasure after the job was finished.

Dalilah did not want to think about leaving, but she knew it was time. She looked at Brad with sadness and said, "I think I need to leave so I can develop more leads. Please know that I don't want to leave, but my client has paid a lot of money for this information, and I have an obligation."

Brad did not want Dalilah to leave either, but he understood. In a hopeless attempt to convince her to stay, he said, "But I thought we were going to Wilmington together?"

"I thought we were, too, but I feel I have all the information I'm going to find here for now. I need to get a broader perspective of what I'm dealing with. Maybe in New York."

"Dalilah, I have this empty hole in my stomach, as if I'd been shot. I don't know if I've ever felt this way about someone."

"Brad, I promise when all this is over, we'll be together again." She felt his strong arms surround her.

She pulled away and went into the bedroom and packed. She was a quick packer. She had learned to be fast from all the traveling her profession required. In fewer than fifteen minutes, she was ready to leave physically, but her heart was heavy. As inconvenient as it was right now, she was in love.

Brad carried Dalilah's bags to her car. He gently hugged her and placed a hand ever so softly on her cheek as he bent down to kiss her inviting lips. She returned the kiss, squeezed him tightly around the waist and began scratching his back with slow, elongated strokes. Both of them moaned in a soulful language fueled by passion and known only to the hearts of people in love. Dalilah hadn't felt this way in a long time. It had to be love because it hurt so much.

***

As Dalilah drove off, the man put his camera away. The pictures would come in handy, should additional action be required. For now he would follow Dalilah as he was being paid to do. He opened his cell phone and touched the memory button.

An older man's voice came through a noisy background, "Da?"

"She's on the move again. I will report when we reach a new location."

"Da. And on another matter. We have complications in Greensboro. Vlad has been arrested. The police are interrogating him. Can he be trusted?"

"Perhaps. But it is his first time in an American jail."

The older man coughed and said in a definite manner, "Why should this worry me?"

"I understand. You have no worries. And the girl?" he inquired.

"Nyet. Forget her for now. She'll be easy to find. You make sure that by tonight, I have no worries in Greensboro!"

The phone disconnected. The man understood his orders.

CHAPTER 27

SERGEANT STEED ARRIVED at the police department and went immediately to CID. As he walked in, some detectives asked if he and Liza were all right. In a small department, word traveled fast.

"Oh, yeah, he never saw me coming. Anyway, Liza is really the one who took him out." Everybody chuckled because they knew Liza could take care of herself.

Steed reached into his top desk drawer and removed his red folder. Every detective had a red folder. It was usually filled with random investigative reports, computer printouts and of course, fingerprint cards. It was the basic interview-interrogation kit placed on the table so the suspect could see a thick file with his name on it. The red folder just sat there; rarely was it ever used. The suspect always assumed the information was against him. The detective never told him any differently.

The detective might pick up the folder and pretend to review a report. This charade, coupled with a few distinguished grunts and groans, added to the intimidation so crucial in interrogations. The detective wanted the suspect to sweat before the questioning ever began.

Steed had received some general information from Sergeant McDonald about the suspect. During the body search, McDonald had found some papers and a picture ID. The suspect was obviously new to the intimidation game and had forgotten a cardinal rule—never, ever carry ID, especially one with a picture.

Mr. Vladimir Rostinov. Steed looked at the ID and a recent plane ticket. While at his desk, he searched warrants and local arrest data. His search proved what he had been thinking. Nothing local came up. He accessed the NCIC, National Crime Information Center, operated by the FBI, for criminal records or outstanding warrants. Similar names appeared on the screen with various aliases. Along with the names came height, weight, scars, tattoos and other identifiable physical marks. None matched Mr. Rostinov's profile.

Steed had one more idea. Since Rostinov had an obvious Eastern European or Russian accent, INTERPOL might have some information on the suspect. It would take minutes, perhaps hours, to get a response. Steed sent the query and picked up his red folder. Before heading to the interview room, he reached into another desk drawer and stuffed an attitude adjuster into his back pants pocket.

The interview room, as it had been called after the word interrogation brought up images of civil rights violations, was located in the back hall of the Criminal Investigations Division. There were three small rooms available, each with a table and two chairs. A two-way mirror was present along with a hidden microphone. Usually the detective would have a partner listening from outside the room, making notes about the interview, keying in on areas of the suspect's story that might need further questioning.

It was better to have a lone detective in the room. One had a better chance of establishing rapport with the suspect. The good-cop-bad-cop routine rarely worked anymore thanks to TV police dramas. Once rapport was established, the suspect would be much more cooperative and confessions would come more easily. If rapport did not happen, if the interview became bogged down or if the suspect grew hostile, the backup detective could provide insight as to which direction the interview might need to take.

This time, however, Steed did not have a backup detective to assist. As a matter of fact, all the detectives had been given special assignments by order of Assistant Chief Allen and Captain Smith. Only the secretary up front stayed to answer the phone. The only police officers in the division were Steed and McDonald.

Before entering the interview room, Steed went to the side observation room where the two-way mirror, intercom speakers and video recorder were located. He shut off the microphone and removed the videotape. Upon leaving the room, he locked the door.

Sergeant McDonald stood guard at the door to the interview room. Steed stopped to speak to him. "Take a break, Sarge. I've got it from here."

"I'll be in the canteen. Let me know when he's ready for transport to the magistrate," McDonald said.

Steed responded silently with a head nod as he turned the dead bolt and entered interview room three, the farthest room down the hall. The suspect was sitting in a chair with his head on the table.

"I am Detective Sergeant Kyle Steed with the Greensboro Police Department. You have been arrested for assault, vandalism and resisting arrest. I have some questions to ask you."

The suspect looked up. Even though his eyes had been washed, he still had a red, irritated look where the pepper spray had left its mark. He said something in a foreign language.

Steed asked him, "Is that Russian? Are you Russian?"

The man simply said, "Da," and continued mumbling.

In an attempt to gain his confidence, Steed asked, "Would you like the handcuffs removed as a gesture of good will?"

"Da."

Steed reached behind him and removed the handcuffs. The Russian rubbed his wrists and mumbled again. Steed sat down across the table and asked, "Would you like a cigarette or a Coke?"

"Da."

"Well, good. When we get some answers, I will be happy to reward you for your cooperation."

Kyle knew the Russian had been trained from birth not to trust the government. It was a social mandate to defy the government. Being born in a communist country with horrible civil rights violations, every citizen was embedded with a duty to lie, defraud, cheat and steal from the government. The obligation extended to killing any government official should an opportunity present itself.

The social structure was so brutal that it created a "kill or be killed" atmosphere. The young Russian was a product of this intellect. Kyle's experience as a detective gave him the insight to know that this kid had an innate disrespect for any government official. He understood him just by looking at him. As far as he was concerned, governments were governments no matter where you went. They might be dressed differently on the outside, but on the inside, they were cut from the same cloth.

Usually Steed read the Miranda rights and had the suspect sign the waiver. However, this was a different case. Prosecution was not as important as gaining information.

The Russian remained aloof and said, "I need to make a phone call. I have a right to a phone call. This is America. I want a lawyer."

Because of Hollywood, people automatically thought they had the right to a phone call. That was not so. They got a chance to make a phone call after their probable cause hearing with the magistrate . . . not before.

Steed said, "I'm afraid you've watched too much American television, comrade."

The Russian straightened himself in his chair. For the first time, he felt uneasy. Sergeant Steed, with his twenty-eight years of experience, noticed the change in attitude and posture. He was patient. He would get the information he needed.

Steed moved around the table and sat next to the Russian, invading his personal space, hoping to add to the suspect's stress level and give the impression that control was slipping away. Most suspects, especially first-timers, would say anything to have their personal space back.

Vladimir was new at the game. Apparently he had watched his bosses and supervisors bully people and thought he could do it right the first time. He was wrong. He did not have the stern approach that came from years of street survival, criminal enterprising and hard-core reality. Steed would take advantage of his weakness and inexperience.

"Is Vladimir Rostinov your real name?"

"Yes, and I have connections."

"Why were you at EarthStar International today, and what were you looking for?"

"I was looking for some American bitch to find out what information she had on a case. Just as you do, finding answers."

The suspect had no idea Dalilah was Kyle's goddaughter and Liza a special friend. "What specifically were you looking for? You know, the sooner you give me the answers I want, the sooner you'll get a smoke."

The Russian looked at him with disdain. "I have nothing to say. My superiors will be here soon to take care of this matter."

It was time to press the suspect. Steed was prepared to do whatever it took to find some answers. "Just so you know. If you don't answer my questions, the FBI will be here to interrogate you."

Steed quick-fired questions as he moved closer, just inches from his face. He could feel the heat from Rostinov's body and see the sweat running beneath his hair at his temple.

"Who do you work for? What were you hoping to find? Who else in your organization is in Greensboro? How long have you been here? How did you know where EarthStar International was located? When did you arrive in the United States? Have you ever been arrested? Why did you hit the woman in the office? Where do you live?"

Kyle saw Vladimir tensing up as he continued his intimidation. This thug probably had suffered humiliation at the hands of bullies all his life. Now, in America, he had found the same, even though he was part of a crime family that gave him the credentials and respect he desperately wanted.

Seeing Vladimir's body tremble as his rage was about to erupt, Kyle assaulted his ego further by reminding him that a woman had kicked his ass today. "You did not accomplish your mission, comrade."

Steed would soon extract justice against the Russian for hurting Liza. He would be ready when Vladimir made his move. Steed reached into his back pocket for a martial arts weapon used in close-quarter confrontations. The Japanese called it a yawara.

As if by cue, the Russian stood and hollered, "Get off me, you fuck!" He threw a punch with his right hand. Steed blocked the punch and drove the point of the yawara deep into the suspect's solar plexus. All the oxygen left Vladimir's lungs. As the Russian made a gasping grope, Steed delivered a well-placed kick to his groin. The suspect crumpled.

Steed lifted the Russian by the hair. With a breathy, low tone, he said, "Now, let me ask again, comrade. Who do you work for, and what did you hope to find at EarthStar?"

The Russian attempted to push Steed with his shoulder, but Steed sidestepped and rammed the yawara deep into Vladimir's rib cage. The Russian emitted another groan and fell to the floor again, holding his side.

Steed was careful not to strike him in the face. That would create physical evidence of abuse, not to mention blood. Steed continued to execute, without flaw, body strikes that caused crushing pain. The suspect looked up and mumbled something in Russian.

"I didn't understand you, comrade. Do you wish to cooperate now?"

Steed lifted the suspect into the chair. Just to make sure Vladimir didn't throw another right-handed punch, Steed struck with the yawara's steel tip into the brachial plexus nerve center, near the armpit. The Russian's entire arm went numb, and he slumped to the right.

Vladimir was helpless, and he knew it. He looked around, dazed and willing to cooperate. Sergeant Steed opened his right hand and revealed the weapon that had paralyzed him. Most suspects thought it was some kind of electrical weapon like a cattle prod.

The small piece of black plastic was made from the same material as the police nightsticks. The yawara was about five inches long and fit into the palm of the hand. For added penetration and focus, two steel balls on each end enhanced its pain-inducing effects. The weapon was ideal for striking the body's nerve centers. Kyle and Dalilah had both learned the secrets of this weapon from her dad.

The Russian gladly gave up all the information he knew. After another hour of filling in the gaps, Steed was ready for Vladimir to be transported to the magistrate.

Sergeant McDonald responded promptly after being paged over the intercom. He entered CID and gestured with a thumbs up. Steed responded in kind.

Vladimir was handcuffed and Sergeant McDonald escorted him to the patrol car. The Russian was quiet and said nothing.

Kyle went to his desk and called Liza. "I have some information. I'll pick you up at 5:00."

"I'll be waiting."

CHAPTER 28

DALILAH WAS BACK in full swing with her thoughts as she enjoyed the wind blowing in her hair. It was time to get some real information about the Russian diamonds. She could think of no one better to help than her college roommate. Laura lived in New York City and worked for the diamond industry.

Leaving the Morehead City limits on Highway 70, Dalilah picked up her cell phone. Speed dial. After one ring, a voice answered, "EarthStar International, Liza speaking. How may I assist you?"

"Hey, this is Dalilah. I'm headed to the Raleigh-Durham airport, and I'm just now leaving Morehead City. Can you get me a flight ASAP to New York, preferably landing at JFK?"

"Well, how is your day going?" Liza said in a sarcastic tone. "Mine is going just fine. So nice to hear from you."

"Sorry. You know how I get when I'm thinking too fast and too much."

"Yes, I do, dear. Now, are you all right? How is Brad? Are you two seeing each other again? He is a very nice boy. Did you find what you were looking for in Morehead City? "

"Yes, I got some stuff I can use, mostly background findings. But it's pretty much a dead end down here. That's why I need to go to New York to see Laura. I need a quick education on Russian diamonds, and I need it from someone in the business."

"Well, do be careful, dear. By the way, we had an incident here."

Dalilah could tell from Liza's tone that it was serious. "Are you okay?"

"Yes. Kyle came to my rescue. But I'm fine, just a little shaken. I wasn't expecting what happened, so it threw me for a bit."

"Does it have to do with this case?"

"Yes, I think so. Kyle is headed over here at five to pick me up. He interrogated the suspect, who's Russian."

"Russian! What do you mean, Russian?"

"He sounded Russian, and he was a young man. He said he had an appointment with you. I checked the book and didn't see any notes you might have made. When I tried to ask some questions, he sort of pushed me down."

"Oh, my God! I'm so sorry, Liza. Are you hurt in any way?"

"No, I fell back into the chair. That's when Kyle came in."

"Why was Kyle there?"

"Oh, we had a lunch date."

Dalilah smiled. "Well, about time the two of you did something."

"Anyway, Kyle said he would fill me in on what he got out of the Russian kid. As soon as I hear something, I'll let you know. Once you get to Laura's place, call me. I should know something by then."

"Okay, Liza. I'm so glad you're okay. I should be at the airport in two hours if the traffic isn't bad. And I know what you're thinking. I'll be careful."

Liza hung up the phone and immediately made reservations for Dalilah on the earliest flight to JFK. She managed to get a 9:05 flight. That would give Dalilah enough time to get there, park her car and clear TSA safety inspection. Liza called and gave her the flight information.

Dalilah hit her memory pad to dial Laura's number. Laura would probably still be at work since she was a workaholic, and Dalilah hoped she wasn't out of town. She did a lot of traveling as Vice President of International Marketing with the Diamond Consortium of New York.

A familiar voice sporting a British accent answered the phone. "Hello, love. I hope it's you, Dalilah."

"It is, Laura. How are you? I must say your accent gets better each time I talk with you."

"Yes, the demands of the profession. I wish you were in town. I miss you so much. I have some good news for you."

"Well, you get your wish. I'm headed your way at 9:05 p.m. Can you pick me up at JFK, or should I make arrangements for a ride?"

"That's great! I wish I could pick you up, but I have a client coming in at 8:00. I should be finished by 10:00, so why don't you grab a cab and meet me at my place? Let yourself in with your key."

"I'll see you there. I need some help with Russian diamonds. I need some insider info."

"Okay, sis, see you around ten."

Last Christmas was the last time she had seen her best friend in the entire world. With her work schedule, it seemed life was moving so fast that she didn't get the chance to spend time with the people she loved.

Dalilah thought about Liza's assault. This was the first time the agency had suffered such a brazen attack. She really needed to make time to be with Liza. Dalilah checked the rear view mirror, but nothing seemed out of the ordinary.

She had to maintain focus on her surroundings and be aware of everything all the time. With the assault on Liza, Dalilah could not afford to be slack or to be compromised in any way. It was definitely time to think like a warrior and to have a contingent battle plan. She would take this time to gather her intent and muster her inner energies. Dalilah reached for the CD player and slid in a Kitaro CD. This was her Tai Chi music, and it would help keep her grounded. Her inner switch had been turned on.

All of her training could come to task on this case. Deep inside, she felt something, and it made her uneasy. She had learned to trust her feelings. Dalilah wished her dad were available. She needed to talk to him, but he was away on a spiritual retreat with Jeanne, her bonus mom, Dad's second wife.

She decided to picture his face and send him a telepathic message. He had told her if she ever needed him, all she had to do was to visualize him and call out his name. She did just that.

CHAPTER 29

A MAN KNOCKED on the door of an apartment. The door slowly opened as someone looked out into the darkness. "What do you want?"

"It's me. Open up."

The young man knew the voice and immediately opened the door. The hallway was dark, but he knew the tone and the demeanor. There was no mistaking Gregori. He was not a man to be taken lightly . . . as if anyone would dare.

Gregori was the shaker and mover of the organization for Europe. His territory had been expanded to include the United States. His job was to make sure Victor had no worries.

***

Victor was the boss of a distinctive criminal organization responsible for a diversified portfolio of questionable and illegal activities worldwide. He was a politician retired from the Politburo of the old Soviet Union. After the fall of the regime came perestroika and McDonald's in Moscow. Victor decided it was time to invest his energies in other projects, mainly those with positive cash flow. Gregori became his right-hand man.

Gregori Petrolovich Novikov had been a young Russian soldier when the Soviet Union was still a superpower. His superiors noted his athletic skills and mental agility. He was soon transferred to Spetnatz, the special forces of the Russian military machine. He learned to be an excellent soldier and was skilled in many areas, from explosives to espionage. He rose through the ranks quickly, and in two years attained a commission as a lieutenant.

His life changed drastically soon thereafter, due in part to his heroic efforts in saving the life of one Politburo member's daughter from drowning. It was early spring, and she had fallen through the ice while skating. Gregori was in the hospital with pneumonia for two weeks. When he was discharged, he had been promoted to captain and assigned to KGB headquarters.

Gregori's talents continued to blossom as he made the rank of colonel within five years. He was on the fast track, and members of the government noticed his actions with much interest. He was handsome, intelligent, and he got the job done. He was soon given the informal name of "Mechanic." He fixed everything, and he fixed it right the first time. No loose ends. No worries.

The KGB went through terrible breakdowns after the events of the 1990s. Older agents were no longer trusted, and newer agents did not have the experience. Gregori was about to retire when Victor contacted him for a position in international marketing. Victor told him it was the least he could do for someone who had saved the life of his precious daughter.

Gregori jumped at the chance to travel. He understood Victor's business perspective and he admired his efficient methods at acquiring the best and the most profitable results. Gregori had respect for Victor. What Victor wanted, Victor got. And Gregori was his man.

***

Gregori asked the older man in the dank apartment for an update.

"Vlad has been taken to the county jail. His bond is set at five thousand dollars."

"Make arrangements. He gets out tonight."

The older man picked up the phone and called for the cash. Gregori sat down after the long drive from Morehead City and picked up the newspaper. He folded one edge of the paper down. Peering over the top, he said to one of the other young men, "Stoli."

The young man nervously poured the vodka over ice and handed it to his boss. Gregori was a purist about his vodka. He drank only Stolichnaya, produced in the Siberian region of Russia. Its smooth taste, derived from winter wheat and glacial waters, reminded him of better times in Mother Russia . . . when he was a true patriot.

The older man hung up the phone. "The money will be here in thirty minutes."

Gregori nodded his head and said, "Da."

CHAPTER 30

DALILAH AWAKENED FROM her power nap as the flight attendant checked seat belts. She had leaned over quite a bit into another passenger's seat, but he didn't seem to mind. In fact, he was disappointed when she woke up. The flight seemed to have taken only thirty minutes, but she knew it was an hour-and-a-half flight. It was an easy trip. She wondered why she didn't do it more often, especially with Laura there.

Dalilah left the plane, thanking the man for allowing her to nap in his space. She didn't have any baggage to pick up since she always used carry-on. She was a light packer, and she could always pick up something if she needed it.

As she left the main terminal entrance to hail a cab, Dalilah stumbled and slapped the pavement hard. A police officer rushed to her aid, but she got up laughing at herself. She stood and took a bow. The crowd responded with a hearty New York welcome by clapping and cheering.

Hazards of being a Gemini, she thought. Thinking of too many things at one time, chewing gum and trying to walk.

After gaining her composure, she took a deep breath and felt the energy of New York. The City was most incredible . . . so alive, so full of hope and anticipation. A cab pulled up as Dalilah stepped closer to the curb. "West Seventy-Seventh, please."

The driver responded in broken English, "Yes, ma'am. Are you here for business or pleasure?"

"A little of both, I hope." She looked at the visor where the driver's picture and registration were located. "Hussein."

"Yes, ma'am, at your service."

"How long have you been driving, Hussein?"

"About three years, ever since I come to New York," he responded with a heavy accent.

"That's great. How about taking me up Broadway? I just love the City at night with all the lights and energy."

"Yes, ma'am, can do."

Dalilah sat back and thought about Brad. He had changed, or maybe she had changed. Whatever it was, she liked it, and she wanted to be with him. She felt safe with him, not just physically, but mentally and spiritually. And she could feel his love for her. They had really connected this time.

Dalilah moved closer to the window as they entered the City. They drove up Broadway, and she smiled like a kid as she saw the lights of Times Square and the busy people of New York. Soon they arrived at Laura's residence in Central Park West, an exclusive neighborhood. She thanked Hussein for the personal tour and tipped him well. He responded in a foreign language, or maybe it was English. She was too tired to figure it out.

She found her key, looked up at the building's façade and then took the elevator to the twenty-first floor.

The condo was immaculate in every way. Laura often had to wine and dine high-profile clients, so her place had to be a showroom. Even the balloons she set up for Dalilah matched the décor. Dalilah read the note.

> Hi, sis. I'll see you around 10-ish. Leftovers in the frig. Help yourself.
> – Love, L.

Dalilah was a junior when she met Laura, a sophomore. They roomed together and became very close. Laura called her "sis" since Dalilah watched over her, but they were closer than sisters.

Dalilah wasted no time in hitting the shower. They'd catch up on the good news Laura had mentioned over the phone. And even though it was a short flight and a pleasant ride through the city, her sidewalk antics made her feel dirty. Laura had called her a clean freak in college. Maybe it was part of her Oriental upbringing. Her dad used to say, "There is no reason to be hygienically challenged in America. There is plenty of soap and water."

The phone rang. "Hi, Laura. I just stepped out of the shower."

"Hi, sis, still squeaky clean I see. I'm there in fifteen minutes. See you then."

"Okay. I'll call for the pizza." Dalilah loved New York-style pizza with pepperoni and extra cheese. It was their ritual meal.

CHAPTER 31

A COURIER ARRIVED with the money for Vladimir's bond. One of Gregori's men opened the brief-case and counted the stacks of bills. "It's all here."

Gregori stood and stretched. "We leave in five minutes. Two cars."

The men moved with purpose as the nervousness showed on their faces. Each checked his semi-automatic pistol and ammunition. Two younger men left to retrieve the cars and have them ready at the walkway for Gregori.

Gregori asked the older man if all the equipment had been loaded into the car. The older man nodded. Both of them walked out. Gregori sat in the rear as the older man drove. The other four goons followed in the second car.

Arriving at the Guilford County Jail on Eugene Street, one of the younger men went downstairs to the magistrate's office to post the bond. After a wait of thirty minutes, Vladimir appeared in the magistrate's office, escorted by a deputy sheriff. The magistrate told Vladimir the conditions of his release and gave him a court date.

Vladimir looked sad as his comrade escorted him to the parked car with the other three men. He got into the back seat flanked by two of his cohorts. He was immediately given vodka to welcome him back and to relieve his nervousness. New at the game, Vladimir accepted the drink and exhaled with relief. He had no idea what was in store for him.

Both cars drove south from the downtown area and traveled along Interstate 85, headed away from the city limits. After fifteen minutes of driving, they found a lonely parking lot behind a trucking company. All the men except Vladimir were familiar with this spot.

Vladimir was escorted to Gregori's car. Gregori was still in the back seat, and Vlad was invited to join him. The vodka was beginning to work on him, as he acted confident that he had done nothing wrong.

Gregori spoke softly. "Vlad, I knew your father well. We worked together in the same section. So, you see, you are like a son to me."

"Yes. My father spoke of you, too," Vlad said with a penitent tone.

"Sometimes those who are new to this type of business fuck things up. Sometimes people who have been in the business for years fuck up. But I am willing to consider your inexperience."

Both men sat in silence as Gregori listened to Vlad's distressed breathing. Vlad started to speak when Gregori looked in his direction.

"What did you say to the police? I understand you were interrogated for two hours?"

"I said nothing to the police about our operation," Vlad said nervously.

"What did you do for the entire time?"

"The detective just wanted to know if I was Russian."

"What did you tell him?"

"I told him I was Polish, as I have been trained to do."

Gregori, looking at Vlad's demeanor, spoke with an authoritative tone. "Then tell me, what did you talk about for the rest of the time?"

"Basic information. My name. Where I lived. Why I was here. Who my comrades were. What I was doing. What I was hoping to accomplish."

"Did you mention my name at all?"

"No, Gregori. Never. I would never mention anything about you."

"Why is it that I do not trust you? I think you're leaving something out."

"The only thing that the detective got from me was my papers."

"Papers? What papers?" Gregori asked.

"My identification, airline tickets and some other papers I had in my pocket. I forgot to take them out before leaving the apartment today."

"Most unfortunate."

"But Gregori, I told them nothing."

"Vlad, I am going to take a chance on you. Perhaps some of your father is in you. This is your first time, and it was bad luck." Gregori knew what had to be done. He was merely reassuring the young man so he would remain calm.

"Yes, Gregori, bad luck. Thank you for being so understanding."

Gregori nodded to the man standing outside the car door. As the man opened the door, Vlad apologized once again. Gregori nodded to the older man driving the car, who reached into his pocket for a pistol with a silencer. He exited the car and pointed the weapon at Vlad.

Vladimir was a failure and deserved to die a failure's death. He was shot in the back several times. As he lay lifeless on the ground, a final shot was placed in the back of his skull to sever the brain stem.

Two of the other men went behind the loading dock and retrieved a fifty-five-gallon drum. Vlad's body was stuffed into the barrel, and the drum was sealed with a steel band to keep the smell from leaking. Two of the men rolled the barrel into the back of a tractor-trailer bound for the Wilmington port. The drum was marked,

CAUTION—MEDICAL WASTE.

It would be taken out to sea and dumped into international waters for a clean, efficient disposal. The cardinal rule of the crime family was: Make no mistakes because you won't be alive to make a second one.

The drive back to Greensboro was silent. Even though the deed had to be done, killing was an unfortunate business, especially when it involved someone in the organization. Gregori retrieved his cell phone from his pocket. He pushed the memory button and waited.

"Da?" the voice on the other end said.

"You have no worries."

"Good. Keep me informed."

"Da." Gregori put his phone away. He reached into the storage pocket in front of him and removed the Stoli. He poured himself a drink as he thought about Dalilah. He wondered where she was. He would do something about that tomorrow. Tonight he would just rest. Perhaps a woman would soothe his tension. Tasha came to mind. He removed his cell phone again and pressed a number.

CHAPTER 32

THE NEXT MORNING, Sergeant Steed went to the Guilford County Sheriff's Department to continue his interview with Vladimir. He spoke with the deputy behind the bulletproof glass. The speaker crackled, but the deputy was able to make out the name Sergeant Steed wanted. The deputy checked several clipboards and finally searched the computer database to double-check his findings.

"He posted bond. Let's see. Last night about 1 a.m. Paid cash. Five thousand dollars. I can't make out the signature. Sorry."

Steed had a sinking feeling in his gut. He knew Vladimir was gone. He would not be found again. If he were alive, he would be transferred far, far away. Steed punished himself for not having been more careful in keeping track of Vladimir. He should have notified the magistrate's office to call if bond were posted. This was the first case in a while that had jump-started his emotional juices. And that had made him careless. He would be on his toes from now on. Too much depended on him.

Kyle made a call. He was sure Liza was already at work. Before she could finish her introduction, he interrupted her and said, "Liza, he's gone. He posted bond last night."

"Do you think he'll come back here?"

"No. If he is alive, he won't be going there. Can you reach Dalilah and let her know to be extra vigilant?"

"I'll talk to her today. She usually checks in around lunchtime when she's in New York. I'll give her the update."

"Okay, I'll see you later. I'm going to put out an alert on the radio. Maybe he's still in the city, and one of the patrol officers will spot him."

"All right. Please be careful."

"I will. You, too."

Sergeant Steed telephoned the communications officer and provided the information for a BOLO on Vladimir. He supplied the necessary facts so all the patrol and tactical units would be on the lookout for the suspect. Everyone knew it involved Liza, and everyone knew about the interrogation yesterday, so an extra effort would be made to locate Vladimir if he were inside the city limits.

After he finished, he sat down at his desk and put his hands over his face. He couldn't believe he had been so careless. This was a wake-up call to snap him out of the depression he'd been in for the past five years. Unfortunately, the price for his mental fog had been his prime suspect. But now he had focus; he had to protect the two most precious women in his life. Kyle had to find his game face.

CHAPTER 33

DALILAH WAS UP early after spending a late evening with Laura. Since the park was just across the street, she walked over to practice her Tai Chi. She loved doing Tai Chi in Central Park. The feel of the place was amazing; its own brand of special chi filled the air. It was as if the park filtered all the chaotic energy of the city and restored it to calm each morning.

Tai Chi felt better to Dalilah when she was near water, so she headed to the Lake where she found the perfect spot and did some light stretching, along with some simple qi gong movements. She liked the feel of the strong stances and slow repetitive movements while performing her dragon breathing.

Before beginning the Tai Chi forms, she took a deep breath to ground and center. She repeated a mantra her dad and bonus mom had taught her:

Something wonderful is happening to me today.
Something wonderful is happening to me today.
Something wonderful is happening to me today.

Dalilah fluffed her chi bubble and stepped into wu chi or opening stance. With a slight exhale, she began. As gracefully as any ballerina, she flowed flawlessly through all three circles and completed her one-hundred-eight forms of Yang Tai Chi Chuan. Her soulful dance emblazoned her auric field with a beautiful golden-white ball of light. Dalilah could feel the pulsing of her chi as it mixed with the peaceful surroundings. Central Park was made for Tai Chi. As she looked around, she noticed a group of older women watching her. They clapped as she finished. Dalilah waved and said softly, "Thank you."

Breathing in the fresh air from the gently moving trees and listening to the distant sounds of the city awakening, she headed back to the condo. Dalilah thought about the wonderful night she and Laura had enjoyed, eating pizza and catching up on each other's lives. Dalilah was so happy for her friend and her new life plans. When Dalilah walked in, Laura was already dressed and ready to go.

Laura was an appealing woman and an immaculate dresser. She had a slender build and was about two inches taller than Dalilah. Laura's blonde hair, green eyes and hourglass figure made her popular with her male clientele. She wore clothing that showed off her bubbled derrière and muscular legs. She also possessed the mental agility so needed in her job. Laura's major at

N.C. State had been International Marketing and Business, and she had several minors in foreign languages: French, Italian, Dutch and German. As a Virgo, Laura was detailed and analytical. Her sweet Southern demeanor, masked by English accent, made her a perfect representative for the Diamond Consortium's agenda. No one there knew she had a beautiful Southern drawl.

Laura saw Dalilah come in and smiled. "You're up early."

"Yeah, you know how I love to do Tai Chi in the park."

"Well, we have a busy day. Grab a shower, and I'll fix us a bagel and some fruit."

"Okay. Thanks, Laura. You're on. Sounds great."

While Dalilah got ready, Laura made calls to line up appointments for the day. As Dalilah returned to the kitchen, Laura said, "Our first appointment is 10:00 at the Diamond Consortium's main office in Rockefeller Center. One of our marketing experts will give you the low-down on the diamond business. After lunch, we'll see a specialist friend who'll teach you everything you need to know about natural and lab-created diamonds."

Laura handed Dalilah a bagel, and both of them sat at the breakfast nook overlooking Central Park. Dalilah said, "I've thought about what you said last night. I think you should go for it. I mean, I'll miss you, but hey, you'll be in Switzerland."

"Yeah, it will be exciting, and I've always wanted to live in Europe."

"You've done well, Laura. Vice President of training and marketing for the European Division of the Diamond Consortium. Not to mention the six-figure income. What's a girl to do?"

"I'll miss you, Dalilah."

"I'll miss you, too. But I'm only a Skype away."

"Well, enough of this. It's not like I'm moving to another planet. We need to get you educated, and we have about twenty minutes to get to our first stop."

They left the dishes on the table. Laura had a very reliable housekeeper who would be in later to tidy up.

The training center was only about thirty blocks from the condo, so they were able to make great time, especially with Laura's Indy-style driving. She really was a true New Yorker in every sense of the word—confident, worldly and like a seasoned cabbie behind the wheel.

CHAPTER 34

THE TRAINING ROOM was located in the heart of the Diamond District in Manhattan. The room was full of eager anticipation as new recruits were indoctrinated into the glamorous world of jewelry, gold and gemstones. The lesson today would focus on gemstones, and diamonds in particular.

Laura and Dalilah walked up to meet the instructor. Laura was acting a bit nervous. A handsome man with dark curly hair in his early forties stood before them, and he seemed quite the academic type. Laura introduced him to Dalilah. "Sis, this is Simon."

Dalilah gushed, "This is Simon. Oh, my God. I am so happy to meet you."

Dalilah couldn't believe Laura had been able to contain herself. This was her fiancé. She had told Dalilah last night that she was engaged to a sweet man and they were moving to Switzerland. Not only was she starting a new job, but her soon-to-be husband also worked for the Diamond Consortium as the training coordinator for all European members. Laura really deserved a life like this. She had worked hard, and now her promotion was her reward.

Simon looked at Dalilah and said, "Enchanté," as he kissed her hand. "I have heard so much about you, Dalilah. You are so special to my Laura. Please know that you are welcome in our home anytime."

Dalilah liked Simon right away. He seemed genuine, and it was obvious by his gentle touch and adoring eyes that he loved Laura. And Laura was comfortable enough with him to use her Southern drawl, although he apparently understood the need for her British accent when dealing with their clientele.

Simon turned to the other people in the room and said, "Please be seated, ladies and gentlemen, and we shall begin."

Dalilah and Laura looked at each other. Without saying a word, they knew exactly what the other was thinking. It was as if they had been sisters in a past life. Dalilah gave Laura an approving nod. Dalilah was going to miss her best friend and confidant. Even though they saw each other only three or four times a year, it would be different once Laura was married and living in Switzerland. It made Dalilah a little sad, and she thought about Brad.

Simon walked to the podium to begin his opening remarks. "Welcome to the monthly training session hosted by the Diamond Consortium of New York. My name is Simon Moscovitz, and I will be your facilitator. Our topic is gemstones. Today we are focusing on diamonds and the production of lab-created diamonds."

"I know all of you are relatively new to the diamond industry, some of you in sales and others planning to open your own retail businesses. I am sure you will find the material today both informative and very much needed for your success in today's jewelry industry, especially those of you who will be working in the diamond side of the business."

The crowd looked energetic and eager to learn. Dalilah was also pumped about the class, even though she kept looking at Laura and smiling. Simon appeared to be a capable facilitator, and he exuded a confident presence even though there were more than a hundred participants. His demeanor made it obvious why he had been promoted to the new training position in Switzerland.

"First," Simon continued, "let's discuss the geology of gemstones and identification. Then I would like to move to the basics of gemstone classification. After lunch we will look into the production of diamonds in the laboratory and what you can do to identify these lab-created gemstones."

The crowd settled in, paper and pen at the ready. Dalilah was no exception.

Simon began with basic geology and identification. Dalilah took notes as fast as she could write. It was fascinating to discover the world of gemstones. She had had no idea how incredible they really were. Then Simon captured her undivided attention with his next statement.

"North Carolina is the only state where the four precious gems can be found. Diamonds, emeralds, rubies and sapphires have all been discovered in this southern state." Simon glanced at Dalilah and smiled.

Dalilah was shocked to hear that diamonds had been found in North Carolina. She knew about emeralds, sapphires and rubies. But not diamonds. She wrote a note to herself to find out more about Carolina diamonds.

Simon then talked about gemstones that have the same basic mineral composition but, due to their coloring, have different common names. "Corundum, composed of aluminum oxide, is the second-hardest known mineral. The diamond is the hardest. Corundum has two common names, of which I am sure you are familiar. If it's red, it's called ruby. If it's blue, it's called sapphire."

A rumble of voices stirred the room as people seemed amazed. The buzz soon stopped.

"Corundum is primarily found in North Carolina and Montana. I am sure that all of you are familiar with the different colors of sapphire. Now you know that rubies and sapphires are basically the same stone, geologically speaking. Another gemstone which may surprise you is emerald. Emeralds are composed of beryllium aluminum silicate, and they are often referred to as beryl. If beryl is green, it's called an emerald. If it has a bluish-green tint, it's called aquamarine. The pink beryl is called morganite. Beryl also comes to us in other colors, mainly red and yellow.

"A note of interest about emeralds. Again, North Carolina produces more emeralds than any other place in North America. The largest emerald ever discovered, weighing three-quarters of a pound, was found in North Carolina in 1984."

Dalilah was in shock. She had never known North Carolina was such a haven for gemstones. She would definitely have to discover the hidden treasures of her home state. Simon continued to dazzle the audience with his energetic teaching methods. He moved constantly with wide arm gestures, heightened tones in his voice, simultaneous use of a variety of audiovisual media.

The morning flew by until it was time for lunch. The audience cleared the room and Laura, Simon and Dalilah walked out together. The three of them engaged in a lively conversation, thoroughly enjoying one another's company. They soon arrived at Simon's favorite restaurant, a little French bistro owned by his kid sister, Régine.

After being seated, Dalilah shared with them why she needed to know about the lab-created diamonds. All eyes were glued on Dalilah.

CHAPTER 35

SERGEANT STEED WENT back to his desk to review his notes. He looked through everything. He felt he had missed something. Then it appeared in the margin. It looked like Gregori. Vladimir must have slipped up during the interrogation and mentioned a name.

As he searched his memory, Steed wondered why he had written down Gregori. The location of the name on his notepad indicated it was later in the session. Perhaps he whispered the name during the attitude adjustment time when the interrogation had gotten physical. Maybe Vladimir blurted out the name or mumbled it when he was in pain. Anyway, he had written it down, so it must mean something.

Steed jazzed up his investigative juices. The passion for police work was coming back. This was how it used to feel when he first started as a detective. He remembered relentless drive, ambition and pure passion for his work. It had been so long since he felt this way. The adrenaline of the chase had come back. It was a big world, and now he had to find someone named Gregori.

Steed punched in the number for the local FBI field office and asked for Special Agent Maroney.

"Hi, Kyle," Maroney said. "Long time no see. What's up?"

"How's it going, Mac? I've got a case of trespassing and assault, but I think it might be more than that. I arrested a Russian kid yesterday for roughing up someone, and he's disappeared after posting bond. During the interview he mentioned someone named Gregori. This may be a long shot, but do you have any info on any Russian crime families operating on the East Coast? Maybe you've heard of someone named Gregori?"

"Kyle, that name doesn't ring a bell right away, but I can run it through the system to see what we have. Do you have any other info on him?"

"No, I'm afraid that's all I have. And Mac, this is personal. I know the person who was assaulted, so I'd appreciate anything you can do."

"No problem, Kyle. I'll run it right away, and I'll check with some of the other agents. Maybe somebody here will know this Gregori guy. I'll shake the tree, and we'll see what falls out. If the Russians are around, we need to know."

"Thanks, and let's do lunch soon. It's been too long."

"Will do. I'll call when I get something."

As Steed hung up, a body appeared inside his cubicle. It was Special Agent Rickard. He had overheard Kyle talking about a Russian named Gregori.

"Hi, Sergeant Steed. Did I just hear you mention the name Gregori?"

Steed was wary of Rickard's curiosity because the two had never been much for either casual or business conversation. "Yes, I did. Why do you ask?"

"Seems like I know that name from somewhere. I can't quite place it right now. Of course, it's a common Russian name. Maybe I heard it on TV or something." Rickard seemed to be cautious in his response.

"It has to do with a local assault case I had yesterday."

"Oh, yeah, I heard about that. Hope you didn't get hurt."

"No, I'm fine. Thanks for asking, I think."

"Well, what have you got on Gregori?"

"His name came up during the interview."

"Do you have anything besides his name?"

"No, but I have the FBI looking into it. Maybe they'll have something in their database."

"Yeah, maybe they will. If I remember anything about that name, I'll let you know."

"Thanks, Rickard."

***

Special Agent Rickard went immediately to his car, pulled out a secure cell phone and dialed his supervisor at the DEA.

"John, this is Rickard. I need some info. Anything on any Russians operating in North

Carolina or the East Coast. The only thing I have is Gregori. I need this ASAP."

"Okay, Rickard. Anything else you need? Anything we can do here?"

"No, not right now. I'll know more when you get that info to me."

Special Agent Rickard could feel the energy flowing with the Russian angle. What are the chances of a Russian being arrested for assault here in Greensboro? It had to be related to his investigation with the diamonds and the heroin trafficking. This could be the break of breaks, and it could keep him from wasting his time following up on dead ends with the jewelry stores. Now he had to be patient until he got more information about Gregori.

Suddenly he recalled a most unpleasant rumor. A Russian, possibly named Gregori, had been responsible for the death of three DEA agents in Hamburg two years before during a drug-smuggling sting. The agents had been called to the scene of a major drug buy. When they entered the building, an explosion killed three American agents along with two agents of the German Polizei. The case was never cleared, and all suspects simply vanished.

Rickard could feel this one. It was right in front of him. He would have to speak with Sergeant Steed again. Rickard needed to know what he knew.

CHAPTER 36

DALILAH, LAURA AND Simon returned to the training center after a refreshing lunch. Laura and Simon were inseparable, and Dalilah could see the love they had for each other. Simon was a gentleman in every way and quite chivalrous. He opened doors, seated Laura and held her hand whenever he could. It was pure pleasure to see such romance, and it was what Dalilah herself wanted in a soul mate. Throughout lunch, Dalilah thought about having a loving partner and wished he were with her in New York.

It was nearing two o'clock, and Simon prepared his notes for the afternoon presentation. "Welcome back, everyone. Let's take a look at our topic for the rest of the day. It is entitled, 'Everything You Ever Wanted to Know about Lab-Created Diamonds.'"

The crowd chuckled politely. There were new faces in the crowd, and many of them were first-time attendees at the Diamond Consortium. Simon put them at ease since many hadn't been to New York before.

Simon thanked the Diamond Consortium for their support of the training program. For the new people, he gave some basic information about the Diamond District. "Welcome to 47th Street, the Diamond District. Most of the world's diamonds, about ninety percent, go through New York City, so you can imagine that the Diamond District is quite a busy place. Forty-Seventh Street is home to over 2,500 businesses related to the jewelry industry. Diamond jewelry is made here, cut here, traded, bought, sold and shipped to every venue on the planet. The United States is the largest consumer market for diamonds. You are on holy ground of the diamond trade."

Dalilah was mesmerized as she watched his energy field. She tried to engage her psychic sense and observe his auric field. It was filled with moving white light, and she noticed a purity and sense of peace both in and around him.

"Now, I'll give some directional bearings and landmarks for those of you new to our City. We are sitting on West 47th Street between Fifth Avenue and Sixth Avenue, or the Avenue of the Americas. We are one block south of Rockefeller Center, three blocks south of Radio City Music Hall and one block east of Broadway. All in all, not a bad location for you to see some sights after class."

Using a PowerPoint presentation, Simon put the first slide on the screen. "The 4 Cs. Diamonds are graded using the 4 Cs: color, clarity, carat and cut. To the average consumer, the whiter the diamond, the better. The clarity of a diamond is based on a scale of eleven grades. The highest eight grades have flaws that can be distinguished only by using a 10x microscope or jeweler's loupe. The third C is carat or weight of the diamond. A carat is standardized to two hundred milligrams. And the fourth C, and maybe the most important for sales, is cut or how the stone reflects light. The cut will dazzle a consumer more than any other element. Any questions?"

A few members of the audience asked questions, and Simon answered with interest and concern. He made eye contact with each person as he walked around the room.

Simon went back to the front. "As you may already know, diamonds form deep within the earth's crust, perhaps eighty kilometers or fifty miles underground, at high temperatures and extreme pressure. Diamonds are made of carbon, highly dense carbon. Remember that diamonds are the hardest known minerals on planet Earth. The name for the diamond is derived from the Greek word, *adamas*, meaning invincible.

"In South Africa, the world's main producer of diamonds, the gems are found in the mineral kimberlite. Kimberlite is a volcanic rock. During ancient volcanic eruptions, the kimberlite was pushed closer to the surface where it could be mined.

"Only three percent of all diamonds mined are of gem quality. Most diamonds are used in industrial applications. Now we can imagine the cost of mining versus the consumer market of supply and demand. With only three percent being of gem quality, roughly two million carats are issued on the market yearly. For every gram of diamonds, twenty tons of rock must be worked. Despite the difficulties in acquiring diamonds from nature, it is still a $60 billion industry."

The audience responded favorably as they absorbed the magnitude of their field of endeavor. Some whispered about the ecological impact of the diamond business, but most of them focused on the $60 billion and their piece of the diamond pie.

"Now we come to the reason you are here today: lab-created diamonds and their effect on your jobs. De Beers, the world's number one diamond distributor, has its headquarters in London and its mines in South Africa. De Beers controls over half of all diamonds worldwide, so you can imagine their concern about the threat of lab-created diamonds. These fake diamonds would impact the financial future of diamond-producing companies and countries."

He paused and scanned the faces of his students. "You will be the front line of defense against this fraudulent and costly charade. It will be up to you to detect and notify regulatory agencies about the sale, trade or use of lab-created diamonds. Your job and financial security are on the line. There is money to be made in the diamond and jewelry business, but not if lab-created diamonds are allowed to flood the marketplace. I know that I've given you a lot to think about. Any questions at this point?"

There was a flurry of hands. Simon maintained poise and patience while he got to everyone's question. "Let's continue. The number one threat to the diamond industry is lab-created diamonds from Russia. The Russians have perfected a system of manufacturing large quantities of gem-quality diamonds in a short period of time, sometimes weeks, at minimal cost. The Russian cubic zirconia, or CZ, is also known as phyanite. It was developed for use in laser optical equipment for their space program, so you can imagine the budgetary strain the CZ relieved when natural diamonds were not used. After the breakup of the Soviet Union, enterprising scientists opened diamond labs everywhere. A few of the labs were destroyed by the new Russian government. However, the more lucrative labs have eluded detection due, more than likely, to bribery.

"Russian diamonds have the same hardness as natural diamonds, a ten on the Moh's scale. They also have the same chemical composition as carbon. They exhibit the same optical and physical characteristics as natural diamonds. To the naked untrained eye, it is difficult to determine the validity of a Russian lab-created diamond.

"This is where De Beers has been innovative in creating an instrument that will detect lab-diamonds. It is called Diamond View. Any questionable diamond can be sent to De Beers and analyzed for purity. The machine validates diamonds by measuring the fluorescence created by naturally occurring nitrogen clumps. These clumps are present in ninety-eight percent of all natural diamonds. If the measurements do not concur with standardized industry indicators, we know we have a lab-created diamond."

Simon looked around the room and set his gaze upon Dalilah. "If we could have a volunteer, I will analyze a diamond to show you that the procedure is actually a simple process. Dalilah, I notice you are wearing a diamond pendant. May I use it for our demonstration?"

Dalilah smiled and said, "Why, of course."

She removed the diamond pendant, which had been a gift from her ex-husband. Simon used Diamond View to analyze the gem's integrity. The process was indeed simple.

"As the diamond is analyzed," Simon said, "the results are tabulated on a computer. The results are sent to you by Internet within one working day."

Simon returned the pendant. "Thank you, Dalilah, for your assistance. Since speed is not necessary in this case, you will receive the results soon at your home address."

Simon concluded by explaining the actual laboratory process that created the lab-diamonds. Much of the scientific methods bored Dalilah, but she tried to look interested.

At the end of the class, Laura said to Dalilah, "We have a couple of days reserved at a quaint seaside cottage in the Hamptons. Join us. You know *mi casa es su casa*."

"Thanks for the offer, Laura. But I have to get back to work. You helped me more than you could know. I'm going back to pack, and then I'm headed home tonight. I'll call you this week. And always remember, I love you."

Dalilah hopped into a cab, waved good-bye to Laura and Simon and used her speed dial to call the office. "Liza, I'm finished in New York, and I'm headed home tonight. I'll pick up my car in Raleigh. Is there anything new?"

"The Russian kid got out of jail. Kyle is looking for him, but other than that, all is quiet."

"Good. Glad to know Uncle Kyle is on the case. I'll see you in the morning."

"Okay, dear. Be careful, and I'll see you soon."

Dalilah sat back in her seat and once again enjoyed the energetic streets of New York City. Then she switched her focus and thought about the case. She finally could let herself reflect on Liza's assault. The uneasy feelings rushed in. She didn't like what she was sensing. She had to get back quickly.

CHAPTER 37

"EARTHSTAR INTERNATIONAL, LIZA speaking."

"Hi, Liza. This is Kyle. How does dinner tonight sound? I thought maybe we could talk about what's been going on. And have you heard from Dalilah?"

"Dinner would be great, Kyle. How about if I cook a meal at my place? Seven sound good to you? That should give me enough time to stop by the grocery store. Do you still drink Duplin Hatteras Red?"

"You have a good memory, Liza. Yes, that's great."

"And yes, I have heard from Dalilah. She's headed home tonight."

"Okay, then. I have one more call to make. I'll see you at your house, seven o'clock."

Kyle called the FBI again. "Hey, Mac. I have another quasi-related matter. You know we have a task-force member from Homeland Security, Special Agent Rickard?"

"Yeah, I know about him."

"Can you make a discreet check? There's something about him, just something that's not right."

"Okay, Kyle. I'll do some fishing."

"Thanks, Mac. I owe you."

Kyle grabbed his coat. He had just enough time to head home, shower and meet Liza for dinner. He thought about taking flowers or maybe chocolates. This really wasn't a date; then again, it was beginning to feel like one. He had not done this in a long time, and he was nervous. A good kind of feeling nervous, but nervous nonetheless.

Kyle decided on flowers. He knew he had made the right decision as soon as Liza answered the door, and her eyes lit up.

"Liza, you look wonderful. I mean fabulous. I mean, my God, you're beautiful."

Liza blushed. "Thank you, Kyle. You know how to make an old woman feel good."

Liza was dressed in a knee-length dinner dress with blue sequins. It had a low-cut top and was slit to mid-thigh. Liza was striking in her outfit. Kyle felt the juices flowing all evening as they laughed and touched.

They had been friends for quite a while. Kyle was ready to make a move. Judging by Liza's responses, he felt she was ready, too. They danced slowly in the living room, listening to a Frank Sinatra CD. The lights were low as the candles flickered. It was a perfect evening. Kyle did not want it to end.

Kyle pulled away slightly, looked into Liza's eyes, and said, "I still cook a really great breakfast."

"Why, Kyle Steed, I thought you'd never ask! I'd love to have breakfast with you."

Kyle and Liza's lips met for the first time. It was a little awkward, but long overdue. They were both out of practice. The passion grew as they felt the outline of each other's body. Kyle's heart pounded so hard he feared an implosion. Liza guided him to the couch where he gently lay beside her.

The years of suppressed passion in Kyle's body erupted with nervous tremors. He placed one knee between Liza's legs as he maneuvered slowly. He reached down to feel her outer thigh. He loved her strong legs and shapely body. He could feel the heat beneath Liza's dress as he caressed her inner thighs. She whispered his name with her approval.

Liza moved over to give him room. She felt his manhood come alive as Kyle rubbed against her hip. Their kisses were full of wanting as they responded to each other as soul mates who had connected for the first time. Liza reached down to touch Kyle, and he signaled his longing with a primal moan. Kyle gently caressed Liza's breast. Her whispering his name further ignited their lust.

Kyle lifted himself up while Liza helped remove his shirt and tie. She unbuckled his belt, while he unbuttoned the front of her dress. Their hands bumped into each other's, but they dared not slow down for fear of disturbing this passion-filled moment. Kyle was amazed at how buxom Liza was and how smooth her skin felt. He reached under her dress and lovingly removed her panties. He did it in measured patience as he stopped every so often to kiss her before resuming his duty.

Liza readjusted as Kyle visually feasted on her feminine perfection. He moved closer and entered her. An uncontrollable gasp emerged from deep within him. A divine connection. A feeling he never knew existed. He searched Liza's eyes and saw the twinkling star. Time had stopped.

Kyle and Liza lay on the couch in each other's arms. It had been too long since either of them had shared their love with someone. Kyle was so enthralled with Liza he never noticed the shadows near the window.

Two of Gregori's men were photographing the lovers. Kyle had failed to notice the tail he picked up when leaving the office. He was so excited about seeing Liza that he thought of nothing else. The two men took their pictures and silently left the area.

***

Gregori waited for the return of the surveillance team assigned to the detective who had interrogated Vladimir. He wanted to know everything about this man.

Even though Vladimir had made a stupid and costly mistake, he had been under Gregori's supervision. Local police roughing up one of his men made him look weak. Gregori could not afford to look complacent or inefficient. Time would rectify this problem.

CHAPTER 38

DALILAH WAS AWAKE a little later than usual. The drive from Raleigh to Greensboro on Interstate 40 had been horrendous, filled with heavy rains and multiple traffic accidents.

She lay in bed and rehashed all the information she had learned about lab-created diamonds. Now all she needed was the delivery method and the people responsible for the day-to-day operations. The Russians were certainly on top of the list as viable suspects, given one of their thugs had assaulted Liza. She would keep an open mind for other players. The diamond business was a profitable venture, so the criminal activity could have many layers.

Dalilah had called the office to check in with Liza, but there had been no answer. She had tried Kyle's office number also, but she got only his voice mail. Liza was always in the office on time. Maybe she had stepped into the restroom. Dalilah searched her sensory perceptions and intuitive field and felt nothing out of the ordinary, so no reason to worry. She was sure Liza would hear the voice-mail message.

It was ten o'clock when Liza stepped into the office. She had never been late before. She checked the voice mail and called Dalilah back.

"Hi, sweetheart. I'm in the office now."

"Is everything okay? I called Uncle Kyle, but he didn't answer either."

"Well, that's probably because he was cooking breakfast for me at 8:30."

"You and Uncle Kyle. That's great. I'm headed for the shower, and I'll see you in an hour. We must talk."

"Okay, honey. We'll see you then."

***

As Liza hung up, a deliveryman entered the office with an impressive bouquet of roses.

Liza admired the two-dozen red roses and inhaled the sensuous fragrance as the young man left. She hummed and left the roses on her desk. She was looking for a vase when the phone rang. It was Kyle.

"Kyle, thank you so much for the flowers. They smell absolutely wonderful." Liza picked up the roses and inhaled again.

"What flowers?"

"The red roses you had delivered to the office."

"Liza, I didn't send any flowers. I was going to, but I just got in. Is there a card?"

"No, I don't see one." Liza was beginning to feel

queasy and light headed. She tried to speak. Her tongue felt heavy and thick. The words wouldn't come out. She moaned. Kyle was speaking to her when the room went dark. She fell against her desk and slumped into the chair.

***

Kyle hollered, "Liza, what is it? Are you there? Liza! Liza! I'll be right over!"

He rushed out of the office speaking on his walkie-talkie. "Car 901, I need a patrol car to meet me at EarthStar International, Jefferson Building, ASAP. 10-37."

"Car 901, 10-4."

A patrol car was dispatched immediately for the suspicious activity. Kyle arrived at the same time as the officer. Along with the building security officer, Kyle and the patrolman ran to the elevator as Kyle briefed the other men concerning the morning's events. When they reached EarthStar International, the door was locked. Kyle beat on the door, shouting, "Liza! Liza! Are you in there?"

The security officer used the master key to open the office door. Kyle searched all the rooms. Liza was not there. Her purse was gone, but everything seemed to be in order. Kyle looked beneath the desk and spotted a rose petal. He looked around. Where were the roses she had talked about?

Kyle asked the security guard if he had seen Liza earlier. The guard explained he was new on the job and didn't know all the tenants on this floor yet.

"Did you see a floral delivery this morning?"

"No, sir, there have been no deliveries this morning. All deliveries must check in at the central security desk."

Kyle's gut began to wrench. This was bad, and he knew it. It had to be the Russians. He picked up his cell phone and placed a call to the local FBI office. He needed information. NOW!

CHAPTER 39

LIZA FELT AWFUL. Her head was pounding. She had no concept of time or place. *How long have I been out? Where am I?* Her hands were tied behind her back. She was blindfolded and scared. She did manage to sit up. She gathered her thoughts as she fought back panic. Faraway voices. Several voices and lots of movement.

Liza tried to move closer to the sounds but found she was tethered. She was sitting on the floor, so she moved around as much as she could to feel her surroundings. Cords led to a metal frame. Liza became very still. She heard no more noises. Nothing.

A door opened, and a voice with a foreign accent said, "Drink this water, and take this pill. It will make you feel better."

Liza did not want to take anything, especially from her kidnappers.

The man said, "Please. If I wanted to harm you, I would have. Now take the pill."

Liza opened her mouth and felt the pill on her tongue. She sipped the water and swallowed the pill. "What's the pill for?"

"It will make you feel better. You will thank me very soon."

"Who are you? Where am I? What do you want with me?"

"Your purpose will be known to you in due time." The man's accent sounded like the young Russian who had assaulted her.

Before she could ask any more questions, the door slammed shut. She heard a dead bolt being thrown.

She tried to remain calm. She tried to focus and noticed that she was feeling better. Maybe the pill acted as an antidote for whatever had drugged her. Then she began to think. Oh, my God! I was talking to Kyle about the roses. He must be sick with worry. Surely he's already checked the office. How about Dalilah? Will Kyle get to her first?

I have to stay calm to survive, Liza thought. She visualized Dalilah. She hoped Dalilah had her intuitive antenna on and would feel her attempt to communicate. The pill had taken away the pounding in her head. She was able to concentrate better. Liza breathed methodically and focused her thoughts while whispering Dalilah's name.

CHAPTER 40

DALILAH EXITED THE elevator to see the anguish on Kyle's face. They hugged, and Kyle filled her in on what had happened.

"What do you mean, kidnapped?" Dalilah asked. "Liza?"

"Yes, dear. And we have everybody, and I mean everybody, working on it."

"But where, when, how?" Dalilah's mind went into overload, racing with random thoughts and pictures.

"It was this morning about ten o'clock. I was talking with her on the phone when it happened. When I got here, she was gone. No evidence except a rose petal."

"But I just talked to her an hour ago. What do we need to do now?"

"We have a BOLO statewide on Liza, and I've sent the rose petal to the FBI lab for analysis. We should know something in a couple of hours."

"Why the rose petal?"

"The last thing Liza said was to thank me for the roses. But I didn't send any flowers. Maybe something will turn up in the petal to let us know who we're dealing with."

Dalilah already knew about last night, but she wanted to hear the other side of the story. "Uncle Kyle, why would Liza be talking to you about roses?"

"We had dinner last night."

"And?"

"Well, dinner went very well."

"I'm so glad you two got together. Don't worry, Uncle Kyle. We'll get her back. Now I know why there was such a bonus with this case. Dead bodies, diamonds, Russians and kidnapping! My God, I feel like I've gotten us into a back-door government investigation. But which government and which agency?"

"Do you know anything about your client?"

"No. Absolutely strictly confidential. That's the way it works. I get the information dossier. I do my work. I make the reports. I send it back. I get paid. Very simple. Nice and tidy. We've never had problems like this, let alone any kidnapping."

Kyle drove Dalilah straight to the police department. When they arrived, everyone was scurrying about trying to develop leads. Dalilah and Kyle sat down together and waited. This was the hard part, having to wait for the analysis of evidence. No use searching in wrong places. The best thing to do was wait. Patience was a virtue all investigators learn quickly. Rarely did everything fall into place as easily as on the one-hour TV shows.

Being a person of action, Dalilah tried her best to calm down and sit still. She would use her intuitive skills to search out Liza. She took some deep breaths and used the imagery her dad had taught her.

***

See the flowing river cluttered with debris . . . just as your mind is cluttered with thoughts and emotions. Allow the debris to break away and begin to flow downstream. Now focus on the river flowing smoothly and clearly. Let your mind feel like the river, peaceful and clear of unnecessary thoughts. See yourself walking along the river as it empties into a large lake. See yourself by the lake's edge. The lake is calm and clear. The wind is still, and the reflection on the lake is clear. With the reflection, you see two skies. Your mind is now ready to accept any thoughts, feelings or instructions.

With Dalilah's mind clear, she focused on Liza. She told her mind and body she wanted to feel Liza. A flurry of sensory probes searched for Liza in every direction. Soon Dalilah pictured Liza. Her initial feeling was calm. Liza was calm. She felt restricted in some way, but she was calm. At least she wasn't injured or being injured.

Dalilah knew Liza would try to reach her through a psychic phone call. She had to be calm enough to receive the vibrations. She tried to feel for a location. Dalilah felt Liza was close, still inside the city.

Dalilah took a deep breath and came back to the room mentally. She went to Kyle and said, "She feels calm. That's good, right? It feels like she's still in the city, but I don't know where."

"Liza is lucky to have someone like you in her life. We'll get her back. I feel she's close, too. Maybe some of that stuff you and your dad practice is rubbing off on me."

Kyle's attention turned to the ringing phone. "This may be what we need. Let's hope so."

CHAPTER 41

LIZA HEARD THE dead bolt unlock. She heard footsteps come close, and the blindfold was removed. The man said, "Time to go."

He had a slight Russian accent, just like the man who had come in earlier. This man, though, had more of a polished way about him. He seemed to be in charge. He helped Liza to her feet, checking her hands to make sure they were still bound securely.

Even though the room was dark, Liza could see enough to note he was well groomed, clean shaven, a good-looking man in his early sixties with salt-and-pepper hair.

"Now, madam, we can do this two ways. I can give you the drug, which you have experienced already, or I can put the covering back over your eyes. I will permit you this choice. After all, we can be civilized about this."

"But where are you taking me?"

"You must choose now, madam. My kindness is only temporary, I assure you."

"Then cover my eyes."

"Very well." The man replaced the blindfold. Liza realized how the blindfold removal had jeopardized her safety. He shouted something in Russian, and Liza heard movement in the other room.

She thought to herself that this was much better than being drugged. She still felt the lingering effects of whatever they used on her. She was led carefully out of the room and downstairs. She listened for any noise to determine her whereabouts. All she heard was a steady stream of traffic moving at high speed. I must be in a motel room near the Interstate, but she kept her thoughts to herself.

Liza felt a pull on her arm and one of the men said, "Stop."

Liza stood still and was lifted into a vehicle. She thought it must be a van from the rolling motion of the door sliding shut. After being strapped in with a seat belt, the engine started. Several men spoke in Russian. She recognized the voice of the man in charge. That was the last thing she heard.

Liza was startled awake when the van came to a stop. Unknown to her, she had dozed off for four hours. The drug still in her system had made her sleepy, but she was regaining her alertness. The car door opened, and a hand grabbed her arm. She was guided from the van down to the ground. It felt soft like sand. The weather was hot and muggy. Liza could smell the salt air, and she heard the gentle surf. She had to be at the ocean.

Liza heard the man in charge say something, after which the other men quickly escorted her away. They led her into a house. She tried to listen for noises, but it was very silent inside the house. Liza felt someone push her down into a chair. A door closed as she sat still and simply listened.

A few minutes passed, and Liza heard the door open. She felt her blindfold being removed. A young man stood in front of her. He spoke to her while touching her face. It was short, maybe five words, in a language she didn't understand.

Her hands were still bound. Liza said nothing and stared at him so she could identify him after the police arrested him. The Russian spoke softly and fondled her breasts. Liza screamed and began to curse him. The man continued his touching and tried to kiss her.

In an instant, she saw a flash of dark metal. She could not feel the man against her anymore, and she saw the young Russian lying on the floor. He was bleeding from the head. The man in charge had hit him with some kind of steel tube. It was the same kind of collapsible baton Kyle carried.

He said, "I'm sorry for the inexcusable actions of my younger comrade. This will not happen again."

Liza didn't know what to say. She looked into his eyes. They seemed caring. He could be someone's father, yet he was her kidnapper. He obviously was not a typical street thug. Liza surmised he might be an ex-military or police officer, or a white-collar criminal.

"Thank you very much," she said.

The man spoke harshly as two younger men ran into the room. They were shocked to find their friend unconscious on the floor. The leader spoke to the pair, and they carried the beaten man out of the room. Liza wondered if she would ever see her assailant again.

The man cut loose her bindings and left the room. As the door closed, Liza rubbed her wrists to relieve the numbness. It felt good to be free, or relatively free. The room was dark, but she had a toilet and sink, so she washed her face and drank some water.

Liza returned to the chair and thought about her predicament. She could not figure out why she had been abducted. It had to be related to the young Russian Kyle had arrested. *But why kidnap me?* One frightening thought recurred. Since she had been unmasked, she could identify her kidnappers. This was not good for her. They would not leave someone behind who could identify them. After she served her purpose, she was a dead woman.

She looked around the room for a weapon. There was nothing in the sink or under it. She looked under the bed and found a short piece of metal, possibly a bracket on the box springs. It was not sharp, but it was the only thing she could find. She tucked the metal inside her waistband. She might be able to use it later.

The door opened, and a younger man brought in a plate of fruit with bread and coffee. There were no utensils she could use for weapons. Liza was famished, another aftereffect of the drug. She ate with both hands like a starving teenage boy.

Liza felt much better after eating. She tried to send a psychic message to Dalilah. She pictured Dalilah's face as she also pictured the ocean. She was hoping Dalilah would intuitively pick up on her location. She knew Kyle and Dalilah were together by this point and desperately looking for her. Liza sent a feeling of calm to let Dalilah know she was okay.

The door opened. The man in charge walked in casually. "I imagine that you are curious as to why you are here, yes?"

"Yes, I am. What do you intend to do with me?"

"You, my dear, are merely insurance. Once we are finished, you will be released. Now, for your boyfriend lover, it will be slightly different."

Heat flushed her body as she became enraged. "Why do you want to hurt Kyle?"

"Let's say it is a matter of pride and honor among enemies."

"But why Kyle? He hasn't harmed you."

"It is a professional obligation. I am sorry. I know the two of you are very passionate for each other. I saw the pictures."

Liza didn't know what to say. *How could he have known we were together? Were we being watched the other night? Oh, my God, what am I involved in?* She remained silent as her entire world fell apart. She now knew this man was a professional, probably trained as a government agent. Liza was careful not to assume he had a conscience. She remained outwardly composed.

The man studied her reaction. He said nothing and left the room.

Liza broke down and cried as the door closed. All she could think about was Kyle and Dalilah. She had no concern for her own welfare, just for those she loved.

CHAPTER 42

DALILAH PACED NEAR Kyle's cubicle as she felt anxiety grow inside her. She did her slow-breathing techniques to keep her emotions in check. It seemed so surreal to think that Liza had been kidnapped. Even though her intuition told her she was alive, she still wished Liza were in the office right then giving her endless advice on love and life.

"Yes, I'll be standing by." Steed hung up the phone.

"So, was that the lab?" Dalilah asked. "Good news?"

"Yes, and they're faxing the results right now. A hallucinogenic agent was on the rose petal. Apparently it is used world-wide from medical to covert applications."

"But how did they learn that?"

"Remember back in 2002 when the Russians stormed the Moscow theatre where extremists had taken hostages? They used a gas to incapacitate the terrorists. Unfortunately, it killed over a hundred hostages."

"Yes, I remember all that."

"The FBI managed to obtain a sample from the incident. They have it in Quantico at the lab. It's called Fentanyl. The same substance was on the rose petal. The Russians have a reputation for using it."

Steed walked to the fax machine as it rolled out the lab results along with data on Fentanyl. He laid the reports on the conference table. Both he and Dalilah speed-read the results.

Ready for the briefing, Steed called everyone into the conference room. Dalilah read the information:

> Fentanyl is an official calmative agent researched for its ability to create mass unconsciousness. A neurochemical compound that inhibits the central nervous system, it can be administered by injection or in an aerosol-delivery component. Fentanyl is one thousand times more effective than heroin. Described as an inhalable opiate, making it a fast-acting agent. Can be used by injection as a veterinary anesthetic. Often prescribed as a transdermal patch for chronic pain management in patients already receiving opioid therapy. Extremely dangerous to children under twelve years of age. Symptoms of Fentanyl exposure: slow breathing and heartbeat, which can result in death. Any toxic exposure to Fentanyl requires immediate medical attention. Naloxone is the antidote, which is a common prescription drug given to heroin-overdose victims to help restore breathing.

The room became silent. Agent Rickard came in. "What's going on?"

Several detectives gave him looks of contempt. Steed told him the main scoop.

"Well," Rickard said, "this is your lucky day. I just got off the phone with one of our agents in the Morehead City area. He reported seeing Gregori Petrolovich Novikov and his gang about an hour ago."

Kyle and Dalilah lit up like a raging fire. Both of them knew Liza must be with them. "Do they have a tail?" Steed asked.

"No, not really. But one of our Homeland Security Agents is trying to locate them as we speak."

Steed contacted Police Communications and requested a helicopter. He informed the dispatcher they were en route to the helipad at the Piedmont Triad International Airport with an ETA of fifteen minutes.

The other detectives assigned to the joint task force went to their desks to pack their equipment. They would rendezvous with Sergeant Steed and Special Agent Rickard in Morehead City at the mobile command post. Arrangements were in the making with the Morehead City police department for task force cooperation. A BOLO for Liza, Gregori and his Russian accomplices was issued.

Steed's face had a determined look. Dalilah followed him. No way was he getting on that helicopter without her. Given the nature of the crime and her contacts at the department, there wouldn't be any red tape blocking her ride.

Once in the car, Steed picked up the radio mike, "Car 901, 10-39 PTI with GPD Air One."

"10-4, 901. All units, Car 901, 10-39 to PTI via Bryan Boulevard."

Dalilah was thinking how her dad used to call Uncle Kyle a by-the-book officer. With all the events happening at once, Steed still followed procedure and notified communications he would be driving with blue lights and siren. Oh well, she thought, as long as it gets us there sooner.

Steed maneuvered the unmarked police car like a NASCAR pro. Driving with lights and siren was a dangerous time for police officers. The general public didn't know what to do when they saw the blue lights headed in their direction. Even though state law mandated that motorists pull to the right curb and stop, people panicked and did stupid things like stopping in the middle of the road or pulling out in front of emergency vehicles.

No worries here, though, because Uncle Kyle was a man on a mission. He got them to the heliport in record time—ten minutes for a twenty-minute drive. Everyone bailed out of the car and approached the helicopter. The pilot had already been briefed by one of the detectives downtown. The pilot was a friend of Dalilah's dad. They hugged each other before she climbed aboard. The engine revved as the pilot radioed, "Golf Papa Delta One, permission for take-off."

Dalilah heard the response in her helmet receiver. "Golf Papa Delta One, cleared for take-off, runway 35."

The vibration increased as the helicopter roared to life. Dalilah remained calm. She looked at Kyle and closed her eyes to concentrate on locating Liza.

Dalilah's psychic impressions came very quickly. She didn't have to do the mumbo-jumbo incantations popular on TV. She had trained her intuitive self to give quick information. All the spiritual growth classes with meditation and Reiki were paying off in a real way.

Dalilah saw a fleeting picture of a house near the ocean. Liza had to be there. Dalilah wanted Liza to know the cavalry was coming and to be prepared for anything. Morehead City was about to be inundated with law enforcement like it had never seen before. Dalilah placed all her energy on seeing Liza's face as she sent her a psychic message.

Liza, we know where you are. Kyle and I are on the way. Please hold on. We will save you.

CHAPTER 43

JOSEPH WATCHED SARAH hug Ben. Even though she was married to an ex-Israeli intelligence agent who specialized in security issues, Sarah voiced her motherly concerns whenever they left on business. "Does he really need to go?" she asked her husband.

"Ben is ready to know the family business and he needs to know it top to bottom."

"But he's my only child."

"He's in no safer hands than those of his own father," Joseph retorted.

Sarah conceded. "Ben, make sure you listen to your father."

Being of middle-eastern heritage was a hard life. Terrorism, deaths, bombings and constant vigilance were part and parcel of their lives on any given day.

Joseph often discussed his irritation with some of his friends at the dinner table. He didn't understand how people complained of mundane events and tasks. If only they knew the horror of war and the persistence needed to achieve security. Most of their friends didn't have a clue about the reality of life and death.

In a sense, they were truly blessed not to have any memories of violence, especially those involving a loved one. Patience and tolerance were the order of most days. After all, Joseph and his family were part of the community, and it was necessary that they seem normal in everyone's eyes. Sarah smiled and waved as they drove away.

Joseph said, "Your mother seems a bit worried tonight. A little more than usual."

"I thought she acted kind of weird, too."

Joseph paid attention to those signs. He was especially keen on his wife's intuitive skills, as they had proven to be valuable tools in his line of work. Just to be on the safe side, Joseph placed a call on the way to the marina.

He looked at Ben and felt proud he was his son. Most boys his age wouldn't be able to handle the stress of the business. After all, most boys his age were home playing video games and complaining about taking out the trash. Joseph knew his son would be a very successful businessman. Maybe one day he would introduce Ben to his real world. But tonight there was business.

The phone rang on the other end. "Hello."

"I'm checking for any recent faxes."

The security procedure for this particular phone line required that it be answered with "hello." The key word, "fax," alerted the man on the other end that a security protocol was being requested. The guest safety officer was in the communications center in the upper room of the jewelry store. He grabbed a red notebook from the file cabinet and initiated his security operating procedures checklist. The man moved with precision just as Joseph had trained him.

The special security system would handle any and all threats to his cover, company or family. It was a simple system where parties used everyday words blended into normal conversation. If someone overheard the conversation or were monitoring the phone line, suspicion would not be aroused. As long as everyone knew the word for the day or week, the system worked flawlessly.

Only Joseph and his guest safety officers knew the words. Having a mind-set for security procedures was the paramount reason Joseph hired only ex-police or military officers. After reviewing the proper checklist, the officer stated, "We are now switching to SATCOM."

Joseph touched star-three, and his phone switched to a satellite link with encrypted digital scrambling and automatic GPS plotting and location. He could now speak freely without anyone listening in. The security officer knew his exact location.

"Are you secure?" the officer asked.

"Yes."

"Prepare for authentication. Say color."

Joseph replied, "Red, 121859, Delta Romeo Sierra."

Joseph noticed Ben's surprised expression. This was the first time Ben had heard an authentication process. And Joseph had never spoken in such cryptic language.

The GSO unlocked the small safe on the wall above the console. The safe held five small plastic cases in various colors. He removed the red plastic case which contained the authentication code. The officer broke the case in half and read the paper inside. It matched the code Joseph had given him.

"We have positive authentication. What protocol is requested?"

"Four SRT. No immediate threat identified. RP at marina parking lot."

"Affirmative. Four SRT. Charlie team. Marina parking lot."

Joseph disconnected the satellite link by touching star-seven.

"Dad, what was that all about?"

"Son, I activated a security call out for our Special Response Team. For our protection, we have a security team on alert twenty-four hours a day. There are a total of three teams: Alpha, Bravo and Charlie. This particular day belonged to team Charlie. All four members were contacted and told to meet us at the rendezvous point of the marina parking lot.

"This is for real? You really did all that?"

"I suppose I owe you an explanation," Joseph said.

Ben, with a stunned look, said, "I've always had a feeling you were different from the other dads, but I thought all kids felt that way about their parents."

"Son, I have always trusted your mother's instincts. You saw how she was a little nervous when we left home. In the business we are in, it is important that all considerations for security be acknowledged, no matter how insignificant they may seem. So this is just precautionary."

"But dad, who were you talking to, and what was that code you used? I've never heard you speak like that. It was like listening to a spy movie."

Joseph didn't feel this was the time to tell Ben the real truth, the whole truth, so he soft-pedaled his explanation. "Well, Ben, I am not a spy. It is just that with my previous experience with the government, I am trained in certain security protocols. I have adapted some of those for our own business purposes. It works quite well for us, and it keeps us safe. I don't mean to alarm you."

As Joseph drove into the marina lot, he spotted the SUV loaded with his security team. Both vehicles pulled around so the drivers could speak with each other. Ben recognized some of the men as the GSOs from the store.

Joseph briefed them on the situation and informed the team that they should maintain security at the mooring and parking lot. He told them it wasn't anything specific, just a precautionary measure. Security professionals all over the world spend countless hours of waiting. This team was no different, and these men would wait and watch as ordered. Joseph had personally ensured that his security teams were well trained and well paid.

Joseph and Ben drove to a parking space, then walked to the yacht to prepare for the nightly voyage. The team leader had already deployed the officers to take every vantage point for observation. Only Joseph and Ben would go to sea. Father and son

DIAMOND IN THE ROUGH

were the only ones who knew the time and place of the drop zone of the cadavers. Joseph's intelligence training had taught him to compartmentalize information. Only the person in charge knew every aspect of the operation.

Boarding the yacht, Ben worked without instruction. His maturity level and work ethic were uncommon for a teenage boy . . . actually, Joseph thought, uncommon for most people.

After some preliminary radar and weather checks, Joseph went downstairs to the galley. He reached for the button underneath a bottom storage cabinet that opened an access panel above the stereo system. Various armaments hung behind the panel. Joseph made sure each weapon was ready for action before removing a .45 caliber semi-automatic pistol. He tucked the pistol into his waistband on his right hip and pulled his Aloha shirt over it. He closed the panel and went back upstairs as Ben completed his tasks.

"Ready to cast off, Skipper?" Ben asked.

"Yes, First Mate. Cast off. What a beautiful evening at sea!"

CHAPTER 44

HE HELICOPTER TOUCHED down in the parking lot next to City Hall in Morehead City. The lot had been cleared as a makeshift helipad. After landing, everyone immediately went inside to the command center set up by the Morehead City Police Department.

Since this was now a homeland security issue with the introduction of Russian criminals and a Russian agent wanted by INTERPOL, Liza's kidnapping had brought together over a hundred law enforcement officers from various agencies. Walkie-talkies were set to a specific frequency for this operation so all the officers involved would be able to communicate with one another. Funding was provided by the Homeland Security Act, which urged law enforcement agencies to share information, resources and manpower for a mutual defense against any threat to the United States.

Sergeant Steed gathered everyone in a briefing room and read the effects of the poison Fentanyl. The room was SRO. All eyes were trained on Steed as he read the information. Every officer was apprised of the symptoms, hazards of exposure and the available antidote.

Since Special Agent Rickard was the Homeland Security representative, he took charge and assigned teams for coverage of Carteret County.

Dalilah hoped that she and Brad would be on the same team. She had seen him at the back of the room but was unable to reach him. With all the hustle of the task force, they hadn't been able to talk to each other. As assignments were being made, Brad headed toward Dalilah, but he was redirected when his name was called out.

"Sergeant Lewis," called Rickard. "Please come up here. Give us the skinny on the layout of the ports, marinas and local beach areas."

Brad shrugged at Dalilah and walked to the podium. He gave a general description of Morehead City's port, beach-front areas, marinas and water-ways. His knowledge of the surrounding territory was essential in helping to locate probable hideouts along the beach. After he finished his briefing, he made his way toward Dalilah, and they hugged.

"I'm so sorry to hear that your secretary was kidnapped."

"She's more than a secretary. I just can't believe this is happening."

"Don't worry, Dalilah. We'll find her. We've got some of the best law enforcement officers in the country working on this case."

"Do you have any idea where she might have been taken? Is there a secluded place on the beach that's not on the map, that only the locals know about?"

"There are lots of homes around here that are really secluded. This beach runs all the way from Beaufort to Emerald Isle. That's a lot of beach-front property and anonymity if you want it. And we also have to consider the houses on the sound side by the Intracoastal Waterway."

"We've got to find her, Brad. I don't know what I'd do if anything happened to Liza. She's my . . ."

Before Dalilah could finish, someone called out for Sergeant Lewis. Brad squeezed her hand and went to confer with Special Agent Rickard again. The assignments had been finalized. Brad was to team up with Steed, and, of course, Dalilah would be with them. Their assignment would be the waterfront and any warehouse locations near the port. Specifically, they were to patrol and investigate any suspicious activities, people or vehicles.

***

The rest of the teams covered Morehead City in a dragnet. Everyone with patrol assignments left the command center. Special Agent Rickard stayed with the support personnel to wait for a phone call. Soon his cell phone vibrated. He looked at the caller ID. It was the local DEA agent who had alerted Rickard of Gregori's presence.

"Rickard here. What have you got?"

"I've found them. I knew they would have to eat sometime."

"Where are they? Do you see the woman?"

"No, I mean I have two of them in sight at a pizza parlor on Highway 70. We're not far from the bridge over the causeway. Two Caucasian males, six-foot, one-hundred-eighty pounds. Both with dark hair, short like a military haircut."

Rickard felt his heart racing. He was so close, and he would get his man. He needed this Russian. It would be nice to save the woman, but he needed the Russian. He would have to be promoted after tracking down Gregori.

"Don't lose them," he said. "We have to find Gregori."

"We have two cars. I don't think they've spotted us yet. It shouldn't be too hard to tail them with all the traffic."

"Call me back when they leave."

"Will do, Rickard."

MacAllister Maroney, Greensboro FBI Special Agent in Charge, walked into the room.

"Well, about time you G-Men showed up," Rickard said. "You know Homeland Security has jurisdiction on this one. I've assigned everyone, and we've set up the command post here. You got any more info?"

Mac replied, "Hi, Rickard. Good seeing you, too. Yeah, I was able to get a picture of this Gregori character. Our friends at the NSA gave us an old military photo of him. I thought we'd make copies for everyone."

"Sounds like a great idea. The copy machine is over there."

***

For some reason, Mac was not very fond of Rickard, or at least of his demeanor. This, however, was not the time to think about that. He did try to dig up information about Rickard when Steed had asked him to. Apparently, Rickard was well connected to high sources in the Homeland Security Department. Mac was stonewalled on several attempts to find out anything. He would have to check some backdoor sources for the real story.

For now, he grabbed a walkie-talkie and called Steed. Each unit number had been assigned a simple numerical call sign with the usual phonetic task force designation of "Tom Frank."

"Unit Tom Frank 25."

"Tom Frank 25, go ahead."

"Kyle, this is Mac. I've got some pictures here of your man. Thought you might like a copy."

"Yes, I would. Where can we meet?"

"I'm here in the command center."

"We're not far away. We'll be there in fifteen minutes."

"10-4, I'll stand by."

***

Dalilah noticed how Kyle had perked up. He was strutting around the office with some papers in his hand. He looked at Dalilah and Brad. "I've worked some cases with Mac. I like his style. I can't think of anyone other than Dalilah's dad I'd want by my side in a situation like this."

On the drive back to the command center, Dalilah used the few moments of silence to clear her head. She felt as if something big were about to happen.

She had to stay centered and focused. She had to control herself and her emotions.

Crisis rehearsal was a mental exercise law enforcement officers did before each call. Every contingency was rehearsed—what to say, how to act, how to react, who, what, when, where, how and why of various scenarios and the action plan for survival.

Dalilah's martial arts training had taught her to review each battle from every possible angle so her body and mind would know what to do. Just like rehearsing a play, she had to know her lines, her actions, when to enter and when to leave. Proper timing was crucial, along with instant decision-making. Hesitation and indecision were fatal to a warrior. Don't control. Be in control. Trust your training. Trust your partner. Trust yourself.

Inside the command center Kyle shook hands with Mac. "It's great to see you."

"Good seeing you, too, Kyle. I'm sorry about Liza and this mess."

"I know, but we'll get her back soon."

"Well, here's the picture of Gregori. It's not the best, but it's the only one we have on file. He's been rather elusive."

Kyle, Brad and Dalilah looked at the picture. Gregori did not fit the profile Kyle had imagined in his head. What he saw was a sophisticated-looking man, dressed in a military uniform and quite handsome. Both Dalilah and Brad commented he looked like a proud soldier, not a man wanted by INTERPOL for allegedly committing heinous criminal acts during and after the Balkan War.

"Mac, let me introduce you to these two," Kyle said. "This is Sergeant Brad Lewis of the North Carolina Marine Patrol and my goddaughter, Dalilah."

"Pleasure to meet you."

"Uncle Kyle speaks highly of you, Mac," Dalilah said. "Do you happen to know my dad? They were partners before he retired."

"Yes, I do. We've met on several occasions. Funny guy, right?"

"Yes, that's my dad. The life of the party."

Dalilah excused herself and looked for the restroom. She walked toward the front door since the public restroom was usually located in the main lobby of City Hall. Dalilah looked at the man walking through the door and froze in her steps. She couldn't believe her eyes.

"Dad?"

"Yes, sweetheart. It's me. Sorry it took me so long."

CHAPTER 45

GREGORI WAS ON the phone with Ivan. The rest of the house was quiet. He was tense as evidenced by the tone of the conversation. Usually he was very calm and cool. The pressure from the home office was increasing.

"I will make the delivery! I understand the importance of this mission to be successful."

"Gregori. Comrade. You have always had my trust since the day you saved my daughter. Remember? I have heard some things. And I am just letting you know rumors have reached me."

"Ivan, I have never failed to meet an objective. When have you ever known me not to finish a job or be disloyal? Never!"

"I trust you, Gregori. You are like a son to me. Just do this one last job, and perhaps it is time to think about a vacation. Take a rest. France? Italy, maybe?"

"Yes, after this commitment, I will think about some time off."

Gregori disconnected his cell. He was obviously still very tense. None of his men dared go into the room. They had seen him agitated before. People died when he was agitated.

Gregori went to the cabinet and poured a large glass of Stoli. He plopped some ice cubes in and sat in the chair. Rubbing his temples, he took a sip. He was tired . . . over forty years of his life dedicated to his country and several different governments. Sometimes Gregori didn't know who to trust, which government was real or who had power. He often felt alone, and this was one of those moments.

He wanted to talk with someone, but none of his men had gained the trust needed to be in his inner circle. He stood and walked to the entrance of the room where Liza was imprisoned. He hesitated to enter, so he just stood at the door.

After turning up his glass and finishing the contents, Gregori turned the doorknob. He entered slowly into the dark room. "Liza. Liza, where are you?"

Gregori searched the room and spotted a silhouette through the louvered doors of the closet. "Liza. I want to talk to you. I will not hurt you. But I certainly understand your reluctance."

Liza did not speak or utter a sound. Gregori waited in silence as he pondered the moment. The alcohol was streaming through his system as he evaluated his need to speak with a hostage. He laughed to himself as he left the room.

Gregori answered his phone. "Forget the pizza, and check the warehouse. Listen, comrades. Ivan has called me with some concern. Do I need to say more? Check the warehouse, and make sure everything is set up. No delays this time."

Gregori placed his cell phone back on his belt and shouted orders. The place came alive as everyone started moving and talking. Urgency clouded Gregori's tone.

In a matter of minutes, there was silence except for the sound of a car starting. Two men approached Liza's door. Gregori nodded, and they burst into the room. One man blinded Liza with a flashlight as the other sprayed an aerosol in her face. She fell to the floor and tried to wipe the liquid from her eyes. They placed a black bag over her head as she struggled. The men held her down to allow the drug to take effect. After thirty seconds, Liza stopped moving. They lifted her limp body. A piece of metal made a clinking sound as it fell from her hand to the floor.

CHAPTER 46

DALILAH CONTINUED TO hug her dad, updating him on the case as they walked into the command center.

Kyle was the first to see them. He immediately went to Dalilah's dad. They shook hands and hugged like long-lost friends.

"It's good to see you, Ray. I'm glad you're here. I think we need your help on this one."

"It'll be okay, Kyle. We'll find her. You know she's a tough one. I pity her kidnappers."

Kyle chuckled. "Yeah, she is a fireball, isn't she? Ray, let me introduce you to some of the fellows."

Kyle shouted for everyone to meet in the center of the room. "Everybody, this is Ray Kim, Dalilah's old man and one hell of a detective. And he used to be my partner until he decided to retire and turn into some kind of medicine man, guru, Kahuna thing."

Everyone laughed and welcomed Ray. A camaraderie existed among law enforcement officers because of the nature of the job. They were the warrior clan. Watching out for one another made people close. To trust your partner or another officer was paramount to survival. No matter where they went in the world, any sworn officer was instantly a brother or sister and a friend for life.

Ray spoke with a southern accent and people often mistook him for Hispanic, Indian or Hawaiian. He had tanned skin, black hair and dark eyes. His jovial personality was housed in a stocky build. He was the type of person who knew everybody, and everybody knew him. Ray's broad smile made everyone feel relaxed and calm. He had obviously found the secret to something in life because he was so happy, and that energy carried over to everyone he met.

Special Agent Rickard stepped up to Dalilah and said, "So this is your dad." Both men looked into each other's eyes and silently nodded. Special Agent Rickard reminded Ray that he was in charge of the command center.

"Ray, where did you get that tan?" Kyle asked

"I was on a ceremonial pilgrimage in Hawaii on the island of Kauai when I got Dalilah's message." Dalilah and her father had always had an uncanny psychic bond.

"When I heard Dalilah calling me, I was almost at the peak of Mt. Wai'ale'ale, about a mile up. The mountain is in the center of Kauai. It's the ancient volcano that formed the island. There's a sacred temple on top, a *heiau*. That's what took me so long to get here. I had to climb back down through the rainforest. I just missed you in Greensboro by about an hour. The guys at the PD filled me in and told me where you were. I drove as fast as I could."

Dalilah was thrilled her dad had responded to her psychic SOS. She was sure Kyle understood about the psychic phone call. She knew the other officers might not understand her dad's gifts. Police officers are a very conservative bunch, so when people started talking about energy, auric fields and psychic phone calls, they get skeptical really fast.

When she was a teenager, Dalilah remembered hearing her father and Kyle talk about the esoteric side of police work.

"How do you seem to always know who the criminal is before the case is even developed?" Kyle would ask as the two men lingered at the police club bar with their beers.

"You'll soon see for yourself. It's something you eventually just know," her dad would say. "You learn to trust yourself."

Kyle was among the disbelievers at first. Now he was a believer, mainly because his life had been saved by Ray's psychic abilities.

Dalilah went to get Brad, and they walked up to her dad. "Daddy, this is Brad."

"Brad, I'm Ray Kim. I see that Dalilah is very happy with you. That means I'm very happy with you."

Brad extended his hand. "It's a pleasure to finally meet you, sir. Dalilah has told me so much about you."

"I hope when all this is over, we can have some time together."

"It would be my pleasure. I look forward to that."

Kyle stepped in, "Well, I think we need to get back to it. Ray, you can ride with me. Brad, you and Dalilah team up. I've already told Rickard. That way we'll have another car out there searching."

Special Agent Rickard ran into the room. "Okay, folks, we've spotted two possible suspects near Atlantic Beach. They're headed toward Morehead City on Highway 58. There's a team tailing them right now. Sergeant Steed, take your team, and assist with the tail."

"Any questions?" Kyle asked. "Brad, you lead the way since you know this town. We'll follow." As they left the command center, Ray grabbed Dalilah. "Sweetheart, be careful. I have a feeling these Russians play rough. Remember your training. Do what you need to do."

"I will, Dad. You be careful, too. And, Dad, thanks for coming."

Brad and Dalilah jumped into the marine patrol vehicle, while Kyle and Ray rode in an unmarked police car. Brad led them on an intercept course. He took a few shortcuts, and they arrived at a suitable location to wait for the tailing vehicle.

Dalilah worked the radio and tried to switch channels since there was so much static. She was unable to contact Kyle and her dad.

Brad said, "Well, that's strange. I've never had trouble receiving radio traffic. Even in a hurricane, it's worked."

They had just reached the marina. Brad put his arm out the window and signaled Kyle to pull up close. They were discussing the radio static when an unmarked police car pulled up next to them.

"Hey, our radio went out. You guys having problems, too?"

"Yes, we went static about five minutes ago," Steed replied.

Dalilah asked, "Do you know anything about the Russians headed toward Morehead City on Highway 58."

"Yeah, we had the eye, but we lost them after we crossed the bridge. We tried to alert command, but all we got was static."

***

Unknown to the task force officers, the parking lot was under surveillance, and they were being watched by Joseph's security team. All four members noticed the cars entering the parking lot. Radio communications were unclear, so they had to activate their anti-jamming switches.

The team leader notified Joseph, who told the team to stand by and not to draw any undue attention.

***

No one noticed the van that drove past the marina. Inside, Gregori held his electronic jamming system. It had effectively killed all electronic signals within one mile. Gregori had been following the police car as it tailed his men. He decided he could take no chances with this shipment. He would not allow any government agents to alter his plans for the evening.

One of Gregori's men in the rear of the van was preparing a rocket-propelled grenade for the tailing police car. He was about to take out the car when it suddenly pulled into the marina parking lot.

Gregori looked into the back of the van where Liza remained unconscious. He would revive her soon. Right now, it was best he did not have to deal with her. They continued to the warehouse. Their shipment would arrive soon.

CHAPTER 47

JOSEPH AND BEN waited in the open sea three and a half miles from the marina. They were now in international waters, and both anxiously looked for the signal from the freighter. There was little talk on the yacht tonight. Something was in the air. Joseph couldn't put his finger on it, but he felt it.

It all started with his wife and her intuitive, worried look. Joseph saw the stress on Ben's face. He knew preparedness would win the day, so he took no chances, especially with his son on board. Even though this was a $10 million mission, it was not worth his son's life. The money could be replaced, but injury to his son was not acceptable, even for his country.

The radio came alive again as the security team gave an update. The team leader informed Joseph that the police cars had left the marina parking lot. That was the extent of the report. Nothing seemed to be out of the ordinary. The police could have shown up for any number of reasons. The marina parking lot was easily accessible and well lighted, so it made for a good meeting place.

Joseph's eyes went back to the horizon. Ben came closer. They sat in silence.

CHAPTER 48

BRAD AND DALILAH headed toward the warehouse district to look for anything suspicious. Kyle and Ray drove to the harbormaster's office to check on incoming Russian freighters.

Dalilah's psychic radar was on high beam, and she felt something very odd. She felt jittery and queasy on the inside. She scanned the warehouse area with her inner sense and felt Liza's presence. She debated whether or not to tell Brad. Dalilah thought it better just to suggest they go in a particular direction instead of telling him about her psychic hunches. Brad was in full-alert police mode, so he might prefer more concrete suggestions instead of her intuitive flashes.

Dalilah looked around as they drove slowly through the warehouse area. Brad turned off the headlights and activated the interior switch that killed the brake lights. As they drove along the dark warehouses, Dalilah carefully shined the spotlight in two-second bursts.

Then she saw something that sent a shiver up her spine. They were in front of the warehouse where she had inspected the medical cadavers. Dalilah knew from her spiritual training that nothing was coincidental. Everything happened for a reason.

Was my visit to this warehouse a premonition of events to come? This was supposed to have been a simple case, just information. A case like all the other cases. But now, look what's happening. Why?

Dalilah pulled herself out of her Gemini habit of internal battles, with one side grilling the other with questions and answers and what-ifs. A flicker of light shone through a dirty window.

"Brad, stop the car. I just saw some light in that warehouse. That's the same one I checked out before."

"Are you sure this is the same warehouse? They all look alike to me."

"I'm sure. See the number? Pier 42, Ocean Drive."

Brad grabbed the walkie-talkie to report their situation. "Marine Patrol One to Tac command. We are code 1 at Pier 2 off Port Terminal Road with 10-37 activity."

The radio was silent. Unknown to Brad, it was still being electronically jammed. He tried several more times to tell the tactical command center that they had found something suspicious and were going to investigate. He also tried sending a message on his car radio without success. Dalilah even tried with her cell phone, but there was no signal. They were cut off. They had to decide whether to continue or to return to the command center for backup.

Dalilah wanted to keep going even though Brad was hesitant. He knew protocol was to wait for back-up, but with no radio, this was not an option. They got out of the vehicle and went to the rear of the TrailBlazer to retrieve their war bags. The bags contained special equipment for any contingency. Dalilah became frantic. She couldn't locate her bullet-resistant Kevlar vest. She pulled out her sidearms and her black fatigues—battle dress utilities. Then she remembered taking her vest out and leaving it in the front seat of her car. In the rush to get to the airport, she had grabbed her war bag from the trunk. She would have to go in without her vest.

Her weapon of choice was a Glock 9mm semi-automatic pistol. The Glock was half polymer plastic and half steel, so it made for a light firearm even though it held fifteen rounds. The pistol had been her dad's duty weapon when he was a detective. After receiving it from the police department for his retirement, he passed it on to Dalilah.

Dalilah suited up with her tool belt, which contained all the instruments used by most tactical operatives. She had pepper spray, handcuffs, a collapsible steel baton, a mini-Maglite and two extra magazines with fifteen bullets each. To the outside of her left leg, Dalilah strapped on her backup, a Walther PPK .380-caliber semi-automatic pistol. It was the classic James Bond gun . . . small, reliable, and in the right hands, deadly.

Dalilah reached inside her bag for two more items. Her favorite martial weapons were knives. She was exceptionally skilled with bladed weapons, from samurai swords to pocketknives. Her dad had taught her the skills of bladed fighting, primarily a lesson in biology. To be an effective martial artist meant knowing the body and its weaknesses.

Dalilah could perform with precision. In her early twenties, she had learned to slice apples thrown in mid-air by her father. She loved the simplicity of the swords and knives. Now, she put a six-inch fixed blade tanto made of 440 stainless steel inside a sheath and attached it to the outside of her right boot. The other blade, a folding four-inch quick-release knife, went on her utility belt next to the pepper spray on her left side. Now she had a firearm and a knife on each side of her body.

Dalilah did a final check of all weapons and tools, as Brad emerged fully outfitted in his BDU in an urban camouflage pattern of dark blue, black, gray and white. He was an impressive figure in his warrior gear.

Brad looked at Dalilah. "Where's your vest?"

"I left it in my car in Greensboro."

"Well, we're not going in unless you have a vest."

"I'll be okay, Brad. I'll be extra careful."

"You damn right you'll be extra careful. You're not going inside without a vest. We'll go back and get backup."

"No, Brad. I have a feeling Liza is close by. We can't go back. We may never be this close again."

"Dalilah! God, you are so damn stubborn. Okay, you're wearing mine. Take it or we go back to the command post."

Brad pulled off his vest. It was too big for her, but she adjusted the Velcro. Brad opened his cosmetic case of tactical face paint. The four colors, green, black, loam and brown would keep perspiration and oils from shining in the night. They looked at each other without saying a word. They knew this was dangerous.

Brad whispered to Dalilah as they moved toward the warehouse. "Stay close when we do our building searches. As we move, you look to the left and I'll look right. Okay?"

"Okay, Brad. Be careful."

"You, too."

They moved quietly toward the warehouse window where Dalilah had seen the flicker of light. Just as they approached a nearby door, Brad heard something and stopped moving.

"Did you hear that?" he whispered to Dalilah.

"No. What was it?"

"It sounded like metal slamming together."

***

On the other side of the warehouse area, Gregori supervised his men. To continue the radio interference, he taped the electronic jamming device on the backside of a steel beam. Gregori gave final instructions to his men. "Keep busy and be quiet," he hissed with his KGB tone. He motioned to two of the men. "Move those crates to make room for the cadaver containers. I'll be back soon." He left the warehouse.

After moving at least a hundred cadaver crates and stacking them ten feet high, the men had cleared an area for the incoming shipment. On the wall behind this cleared area, they painted a diagonal cross. These lines marked the spot where the forklift driver was to place the special containers.

The forklift driver had been on the payroll for quite a while and was well paid. To ensure his allegiance, Gregori had pictures of the driver's children, and he knew which schools they attended. The driver would not disappoint him.

The Russian men stopped to take a break and a smoke. They walked over to a crate Gregori had prepared earlier. He left specific instructions that the air hole be unobstructed at all times. They checked the air hole with a casual glance.

***

Inside, Liza faded in and out of consciousness. She was cold, and everything seemed out of focus. She was very nauseated. Her arms and legs were confined, and all she could do was breathe. Some sort of tube was attached to her mouth, and through it she was able to breathe. Everything around her glowed a hazy green. *Where am I? Am I dead? I feel so tired.*

The Russians could not resist the temptation to look one more time. They had pried open the crate marked MEDICAL CADAVER and saw the kidnapped woman. Liza saw fuzzy images of men. Liza could hear men laughing, but they seemed so far away.

CHAPTER 49

KYLE AND RAY introduced themselves to the harbormaster and apprised him of the urgency of the situation. He was more than cooperative with their requests to see all manifests and reports of incoming cargo and freighters for the past twenty-four hours. Kyle sifted through the logs with Ray's help.

"Have any Russian ships docked recently?" Kyle asked.

"None during my shift. And I was working last night, too. We really don't know the registry of the ships until they enter the port area. Now, you boys may want to check with the Coast Guard. I believe the new rules of Homeland Security require all ships entering the USA to give notification seventy-two hours prior to arriving in port. So the Coast Guard may know about incoming cargo ships with Russian registry. I'd let you use my phone, but it went down about an hour ago. So did my radio. I don't believe this has ever happened. Who knows? I guess Mother Nature and the sea salt take their toll on everything."

"How can we get to the Coast Guard station?" Ray asked.

"Well, it's only about fifteen minutes away. Take Highway 58 to Fort Macon State Park. You can't miss it. I'm sure they'll be able to help you."

"Thanks for the info. When the phones come back on line, how about calling this number at the task force command center. Relay any information on Russian ships."

"I will. More than happy to help out the police."

Kyle and Ray sped along Highway 58 to the Coast Guard station. Ray tried the car radio, walkie-talkie and Kyle's cell phone without success. Ray did not like the situation. He and Kyle discussed the odds of all three methods of communication having catastrophic failure. They agreed that the odds were very high indeed, especially without any influencing weather conditions such as lightning, solar flares or high winds.

Ray had experience with electronic jamming devices from his training as an Air Force Security Police Officer. The Air Force, of course, had anti-jamming equipment. Kyle and Ray did not. They would have to rely on their training, experience and good old-fashioned luck.

The fog covered the highway, especially near the low-lying areas by the waterway. Ray checked with his intuitive sense to search the surrounding area. He didn't like what he felt. Something was not right. He felt like they were being watched.

Out of nowhere, a large truck slammed into the rear of the vehicle, pushing them toward a low bridge. The car slammed through the guardrail on Kyle's side and tumbled down an embankment. Kyle was unconscious from the impact. Although it felt like an eternity, the car stopped after a few seconds with a huge splash into the Intracoastal Waterway.

Ray was tossed through the side window into the water. On high alert, ready to exit the vehicle in a split second, he had not been belted in. Saltwater burned his eyes as he struggled to the surface. He had to get to Kyle. The tide was going out, and the current had carried Ray several hundred yards from the car. He swam as hard as he could toward land.

Ray finally worked his way through the razor-sharp oyster beds to stable soil. He could see the partially submerged headlights shining under the surface of the water. Through the parting fog, he saw two men carrying someone away from the vehicle. Ray was relieved to know that Kyle was being rescued. He looked for a way to reach the rescue party, but the fog and darkness made it difficult. He also had to contend with the muck and dense vegetation. He tried to yell to the rescue team, but the wind carried his voice in the opposite direction.

After he reached a high point in some scrub brush, he saw two men holding Kyle; a third punched him in the stomach.

Ray was infuriated. They weren't the rescue team. *We've been targeted. That's why I felt we were being watched.*

He made his way closer to Kyle. He stayed near the bushes for concealment. He was downwind, and the noises he made couldn't be heard. Ray was within fifty yards when he saw Kyle's limp body being shoved into the trunk of a car. Kyle must still be alive. Otherwise, why would they take him? The large truck and the car drove off in the same direction.

Ray wanted to search the wreckage for his pistol, which had come out of its holster. He hoped it was still in or near the car. The strong current had sucked the car deeper into the water until the taillights were barely visible. The seawater had killed the car battery. It was total darkness except for a few distant street lights. He made one final dive to retrieve the rechargeable Maglite fastened to the floorboard. Ray emerged with the flashlight and found a path to the street.

The assailants had chosen a perfect ambush site. It was out of the way with no homes nearby. Since Ray was unsure of the distance to the Coast Guard station, he started jogging at a fair pace back to Morehead City. At least that was the direction in which Kyle had been taken.

**

Gregori's instinct to have Kyle tailed by his men had paid off. He and Detective Sergeant Kyle Steed had an appointment to settle a score, and the appointment would take place tonight. With the shipment en route and all the loose ends nicely tied up, he would soon have riches and power to finance his own business. Gregori had instructed his men to take the sergeant to the warehouse where Liza was being held. There were to be no more assaults on the detective until he arrived.

Gregori drove inland. He had an errand to run before the night was over. He headed to the country club area in Morehead City. He pulled into a driveway and checked his appearance in the mirror before approaching the house. An attractive woman in her mid-forties answered the door.

"Yes, may I help you?"

"Ms. Davidson. I'm afraid there has been an accident. Your husband is all right, but your son has been taken to the emergency room. I'm not aware of the extent of his injuries, but Mr. Davidson said to transport you there as soon as possible."

Gregori's words had given Sarah the shock he intended. She was white and rigid. Fear covered her entire face and body posture. Sarah regained her composure and leaned against the door.

"Let me grab my things," she said. "Oh, my God. Oh, my God."

Gregori was surprised that Sarah went with him so easily. She had obviously not followed security protocol, leaving with him without so much as a phone call. That would be her mistake. He knew that a mother's grief for her child superseded thoughts of self-preservation.

Sarah sat in the back seat where she was accustomed to sitting when she had a driver. She pulled out a tissue. Gregori looked into the rearview mirror and saw her crying. He reached under his jacket and removed an aerosol canister. He quickly sprayed the mist into Sarah's face.

She coughed and tried to grab the door handle, but her motor functions failed. She became still in a matter of seconds with only slow, shallow breathing. As she faded away, she whispered, "Ben."

Gregori drove slowly away so no one would notice his presence. Now the evening was almost complete. He would drive the Mossad agent's wife to the warehouse and have her packaged and ready for shipment. Not only would he have his shipment of heroin, but now he would have the means by which to negotiate an additional payment in diamonds. Russian diamonds.

CHAPTER 50

DALILAH AND BRAD listened for another minute before moving toward the entrance. Hearing no more noises, they looked at each other and moved toward the door. Dalilah pointed to the hinges on the door. They were on the outside, allowing the door to open outward.

Dalilah had a flash of memory about her first lesson on the secret of doors and hinges. She had been seven years old and playing hide and seek with her dad. He was hiding behind a closet door. Dalilah tried as hard as she could to open the door by pushing it in.

After several minutes, her dad came out of the closet and explained to her that the door could not open to the inside because the hinges were on the outside. From that point on, Dalilah always looked at door hinges to determine which way a door opened.

Brad whispered, "Ready? Remember, you look left and I'll take right."

She gave a thumbs-up sign. Both Dalilah and Brad had a firearm in the right hand and a Maglite in the left. Brad pulled the door open. It creaked from years of stress and the salt air. Brad went in first and ducked to the right, taking a low, crouched position.

The warehouse was dark and huge. Most of the buildings along this part of the port were large, some with a million square feet. Dalilah entered behind Brad and took a low position to the left of the door. Both were careful not to silhouette themselves against the window.

Even though both of them had flashlights, they did not use them right away. Dalilah's dad had taught her early in life about using flashlights when they played hide and seek at night outdoors. She recalled the lesson as if it had happened yesterday.

Flashlights are not as tactical as most people think. In movies or TV shows, the officers shine their flashlights everywhere. Not so when your life depends on it. When a flashlight is turned on, unless you shine the beam directly onto the dirtbag, he will see the light before you see him. In a dark room, the flashlight gives away the officer's location. That means the bad guy knows where the officer is, and the officer is placed at a disadvantage.

Brad had obviously had the same training at the police academy, since he also kept his flashlight off. Dalilah sifted through all the lessons she had been taught about tactical operations. She moved silently, thanks to her physical conditioning and martial arts training.

She and Brad began their methodical search for the noise and flicker of light she had seen earlier. They moved along the interior perimeter of the building. As they moved, Dalilah continued to see flashes of Liza's face. She has to be in here or at least close by. Liza, I'm here. I'll find you.

A sudden noise brought Brad and Dalilah to an instant halt. They listened for the direction of the sound. Dalilah pricked her ears for clarity. She could hear someone talking on the far side of the warehouse. She and Brad moved carefully as they closed in on their target. Dalilah took small steps as she felt the floor beneath her feet, ensuring that she not step on anything. Thanks to her practice of Tai Chi, which developed balance, she was able to lightly touch the floor before putting all her weight down on one foot.

Dalilah noticed how Brad moved with precision and agility, despite his tall, muscular frame. He was coordinated and trained religiously with weights along with a daily two-mile run. Once a Marine, always a Marine.

Dalilah and Brad positioned themselves closer to the men. They heard the men speaking, but it was difficult to hear what they were saying. Dalilah listened intently. Then she heard it. They were speaking Russian or some Slavic language.

Dalilah tried to signal Brad that the men were Russian, but she couldn't think of a hand symbol. She tried to move closer to Brad but wasn't able to locate a safe spot. The Russians were using a small lamp that gave off just enough light for her to search her surroundings. She was able to see the large containers next to her. They were emblazoned with several words in many languages. Finally, she stopped moving and read the English on one of the crates: MEDICAL CADAVERS.

CHAPTER 51

BRAD MOVED CLOSER to Dalilah's position, where he heard the men speaking more clearly and his signals could be better seen. He too, thought it was Russian or some Eastern European language. Dalilah peered through the spaces between the crates. Brad saw only two men and gave Dalilah the hand signal by holding up two fingers. He signaled they would confront the men on the count of three. He pointed for Dalilah to come in from the side to flank their position while he made a frontal approach.

On three, they both jumped into position. Brad shouted and shined his flashlight in their faces. "Marine Patrol. Hands up! Hands up! Now!"

The two Russians placed their hands on their heads and spoke to each other in Russian. They seemed confused and unsure about what to do.

Brad's voice filled the entire warehouse. "Hands up! Don't move! Don't move!"

The Russians repeated in broken English, "Okay. Okay." Then they talked to each other in Russian.

"No talking," Brad shouted. "Down to the ground. Now!"

Brad moved closer to the men as Dalilah came from the side and shined her flashlight. The Russians jumped back with a start. As the men continued standing, Brad approached and struck one man's shoulder with his elbow, sending him to the ground. The other man quickly went down voluntarily.

Brad motioned for Dalilah to take his place. She stood at their heads with her pistol and flashlight pointed at them. Brad performed a security sweep. When he returned, he knelt down and patted down each man. They didn't have any weapons or identification. Brad attempted to communicate with them, but they answered in Russian.

He handcuffed the two men for transport back to the command center. If nothing else, they shouldn't have been inside the warehouse. Dalilah told Brad she was taking a look as she pointed to two medical cadaver crates side by side on top of a large table. One of the containers was closed, but a white tube extending upward had been taped to the top. Two cadavers lay on the floor. The other container was empty except for missing pieces of the green sealant.

Dalilah approached the older man, who might have been in his early fifties. "What are you doing with the bodies?"

The man replied in Russian and shrugged his shoulders. The younger man, twenty-something with blonde hair and tattoos on each arm, also replied in Russian and laughed. Brad moved in to adjust his attitude when the lamp exploded. The room went dark.

Brad and Dalilah were temporarily blinded as they crouched down, hoping to establish their night vision quickly. The two Russians shouted as Brad and Dalilah huddled together to regroup. Brad and Dalilah placed their backs against some crates as their night vision came into focus. They could see the outside street lighting coming in from an open door.

"What was that?" Dalilah asked Brad.

"I don't know. I didn't see anything."

Brad was listening for any noise when he heard a suppressed gunshot. The crate next to Dalilah splintered violently and sent wooden pieces into their faces. She ducked and did a body roll as she moved farther away from Brad.

Brad responded with gunfire in the general direction of the Russian men. Dalilah stood to make her way back to Brad. Another shot hit the crate next to her head. She hit the floor and low-crawled in the other direction, which created a greater chasm between her and Brad.

Unable to identify any targets in the darkness, Brad didn't fire anymore, especially since he wasn't sure of Dalilah's exact position. He knew random shooting wasted ammunition and heightened the chances of friendly fire. Brad's tactical training kicked into high gear. Shoot-move-communicate.

CHAPTER 52

DALILAH HESITATED TO call for Brad for fear of giving away her position. She moved in the direction where she had last seen him. A loud shot rang out as Dalilah heard a ricochet. It sounded as if it came from the direction of the Russian men. She could hear them speaking loudly, and it sounded like they were moving. Somehow they must have gotten out of their handcuffs, perhaps by the man who shot the lamp.

Dalilah crouched, ready to move again, when the crate exploded next to her head. *How is someone seeing me? I don't see a thing.*

"Dalilah, are you okay?" Brad asked in a hushed whisper.

"Yes." Dalilah stayed low and quickly moved to a spot away from the crates. She tucked herself between two steel beams with her back against the wall. She listened for movement, but there was silence. Dalilah used her intuitive sense as she scanned the area. Someone was close. Was it Brad? Or was it one of the Russians?

She bristled when a shape passed in front of her twenty feet away. She remained in a crouched position. Her pistol was extended ready to fire in any direction. A red dot appeared on her chest—a laser dot used for target sighting.

"No!" Brad shouted. The bullet slammed into his side as he covered Dalilah's body. Brad fell to the floor on top of Dalilah. He did not move.

"Brad. Are you all right? Oh, my God. Brad! Brad!"

CHAPTER 53

FLASHLIGHT BEAMS SHOWERED Dalilah's face. She saw the silhouettes of three men. Brad was barely breathing and blood trickled from his upper left rib cage. She tried to seal the hole with her hand. The young Russian laughed and said something.

One of the men standing over her removed his night vision goggles. It was the man who had been tracking her for the past week. Speaking in an accented but otherwise perfect English, he said, "Miss Smith, I've been waiting to meet you in person. I am Gregori. I have known you for some time."

Gregori said something in Russian. The older man picked Dalilah up and moved her to a metal folding chair. He handcuffed her hands behind her. The younger man replaced the bulb in the lamp and moved the light closer, illuminating Gregori's face. He sat in a chair opposite Dalilah, close enough to invade her personal space.

"Miss Smith, I can't afford to have you meddle in my business any longer. After tonight, I will retire. Please understand that nothing will prevent me from doing my job. Nothing! Your boyfriend is near death. Your secretary and her lover are going on a trip."

"What have you done to Liza and Kyle?"

"Nothing so far. Merely detaining them. If all goes as planned, the three of you will see one another very soon. Your purpose will have been served."

"You bastard. The police will be here any minute. You won't get away with this."

"But Miss Smith, I already have."

Gregori gave an order to the younger man. He left the building and came back carrying a body over his shoulders. It was a woman. He placed her on the table.

"Liza. Is that Liza?"

"No, Miss Smith. It is none of your concern. Please keep quiet, or I will gag you."

Gregori shouted to his men. They lifted the woman and placed her in the cadaver crate. It was the same empty crate Dalilah had seen earlier. Now she knew what Gregori was doing. After the men packed the green gelatin around the woman's body, they affixed a plastic tube for breathing. The other crate had to have Liza in it. But Gregori mentioned Uncle Kyle. Where is he? Dalilah looked around the room for another crate, but she didn't see one. But Dad was with Uncle Kyle. Where is Dad?

"You have to help Brad," she begged. "He's bleeding. He needs a doctor."

"He is a fine specimen of young America. He's strong. At least I hope so for your sake. Delay me no further, and you will have help for your boyfriend. Continue bothering me, and it will take longer for me to do my work. It's up to you, Miss Smith. His life rests in your hands."

Dalilah remained silent. When no one was watching, she reached for a key inside her back pants pocket. The younger Russian had not searched her thoroughly. After he found her backup pistol and one knife, he stopped searching. He had missed her handcuff key and boot knife. She would be patient and wait for the right moment to attack.

CHAPTER 54

HE SIDE DOOR to the warehouse opened. Two of Gregori's men brought in another person. Dalilah strained in the low light to see who it was. As the two Russians dragged the man closer, she saw Uncle Kyle.

"What did you do to him, Gregori?"

"Don't worry, Miss Smith. He is fine. He doesn't even know where he is. I gave him something to relax him for his upcoming trip."

Dalilah noticed his shallow breathing. It had to be the Fentanyl. She tried to speak to him, but he was unresponsive.

"Miss Smith, you are wasting your time. He's probably on a deserted island with his lover," Gregori said. "I promise you he's in no pain."

All four of Gregori's men grabbed a cadaver crate and placed it on the floor next to the table. One of them pried open the container, and the others removed the green gel. The cadaver was removed and pushed under the table.

***

Gregori ordered two men to pick up the crate that contained Liza. The man who had been beaten earlier for assaulting Liza mumbled something under his breath; the other man laughed. They carried the crate outside and loaded it into the van. The other two carried the crate that contained the woman Gregori had brought in earlier. They loaded her next to Liza. Two men stayed with the van while the other two went back to the warehouse.

Speaking Russian, Gregori gave final orders to his young comrades. "Seal the detective sergeant in the crate. Mix his crate in with the others so no one will find him. There will be no need for a breathing tube. He won't last long. Before you leave, kill the girl and the young American hero. This is a simple task. You want to be a part of the family. Then don't fuck this up."

***

Dalilah didn't know what Gregori had said, but when both of the men looked at her, she had an ominous, chilled feeling. She had to do something. She had already freed her right hand from the handcuffs.

Gregori walked toward her. "Such a shame, Miss Smith. If only we could have met under different circumstances. Both of us are engaged in the same line of work. We both work for other people, providing a service for money. Perhaps we could have been colleagues. Who knows? But I'm afraid our relationship will end here tonight. It is nothing personal. I have a mission, and it will be completed. You can appreciate my position. Yes?"

"I don't kidnap and kill people, Gregori. We are nothing alike. What are you doing with Liza, the other woman and Kyle? If you harm them, I will find you!"

"Ah, such spirit! Such idealism. Still defiant. If only I could instill such passion into my men. It's been a pleasure, Miss Smith."

Gregori answered his cell phone. "Da . . . Da. On time . . . Da."

CHAPTER 55

REGORI PLACED HIS phone back on his hip and said something as he left the building. His men replied and again looked at Dalilah. Then they placed Kyle in the cadaver crate. Dalilah saw his face. He had been beaten. Lucky for him that he was drugged and didn't feel anything. The Russians threw the cadaver gel on top of him in large chunks. One of them had to forcibly hold the lid down as the other man nailed it shut.

Dalilah noticed they had not connected a breathing tube. Hopefully there were air pockets inside Kyle's crate since the two men were not careful in how they packed the gel. But Uncle Kyle would not last long. She had to do something, and it had to be now. She looked over at Brad. He was still face down, not moving. He was breathing, but it was labored and slow.

After sealing Kyle's crate, the men turned toward Dalilah. They pulled out their pistols and walked past her toward Brad. One of the men rolled Brad over so he faced up. Brad moaned as he was moved. The Russians spoke to each other. One of the men placed his gun barrel against Brad's forehead.

"Hey, tough guy, why don't you come after me first?" Dalilah shouted. "Leave him alone. He's almost dead anyway. Why not have some fun with me? Who's going to know? I'm sure you plan to kill me anyway. Right?"

The Russian holding the gun barrel against Brad's forehead looked over at Dalilah. He was the one who had been punished by Gregori for touching Liza. He had a score to settle with American women, and Dalilah would restore his pride. He left Brad and approached Dalilah. He put his face directly in front of Dalilah's and sneered.

He moved closer to kiss her. Dalilah flinched and spit in his face. Instinctively, the man drew back his hand she thought to backhand her. Instead, he moved behind her and grabbed her hair. He forced her from the chair and made her kneel on the concrete. The young Russian spoke loudly with an air of bravado. He was in control. Dalilah managed to keep her hands together as if they were still handcuffed.

The Russian whispered something in her ear and rubbed her face with his pistol. Then he pressed the side of the pistol against the back of her head. Dalilah could feel the pressure, and she pushed back. She wanted to know the gun's exact location.

The other man stood back. Dalilah counted on his complacent attitude. He slumped against the wall. He looked tired, and he'd probably seen this type of activity many times. He pulled out his cigarettes. With the low lighting and her viewpoint, Dalilah was the only one who noticed the shadow passing behind them.

She kept her cool as she maneuvered her hand slowly toward the Japanese tanto on the outside of her lower right leg. She slowly moved her pant leg up to reveal the rubber handle of the knife. The Russian was getting bolder, and she could feel more pressure from his gun against her head. With his free hand, he reached for Dalilah's breasts and fondled them while he spoke to her. The smoking man perked up. He threw down his cigarette and headed toward Dalilah.

Dalilah pushed back so the pistol was tight against her head. Then she made her move. She turned her head quickly to the right, and the man fell forward. Dalilah removed the knife from the sheath and spun to the right. With a backhand thrust, she drove it deep into the back of the Russian's thigh. The man never saw the blade. The pain was evident on his face. His eyes widened, his face contorted and his mouth opened as the knife's tip slammed into his femur. Dalilah twisted her wrist ninety degrees down and up, maximizing tissue damage and severing all blood vessels in the wound.

As she ripped the knife from the back of his leg, the Russian shouted in agony. He turned to the right with his pistol. Dalilah spun back to the left, blocked his arm with one hand and made an upward slice to his wrist. The design of the tanto easily penetrated the wrist's tendons, muscles and bones. The Russian's hand, almost cut in two, dangled in mid-air as the pistol fell to the floor. Dalilah stood and executed a shin kick to the wounded thigh, making direct contact with the common peroneal nerve center on the side of the leg.

The young Russian buckled as his leg collapsed. Dalilah pulled him closer and drove the tanto deep into his throat, severing the trachea as the Russian screamed silently. She twisted the blade several times. The arterial splash let her know that he would soon be dead.

The other Russian stood in panic. The events had unfolded in seconds. As he raised his gun to shoot, a dark object crashed down on his arm, causing the bone to snap. His gun fell to the floor as Dalilah saw a hand deliver a deathblow to the side of his neck.

Ray had emerged from the shadows and struck the man with a hammer fist to the vagus nerve center, causing his heart and lungs to spasm. The Russian gasped for air, but it was too late. The precise pressure point strike had shut down his cardiovascular system. He lay dead on the warehouse floor.

Ray and Dalilah hugged. "Are you hurt?" Ray asked.

"No, I'm all right. Where did you come from?"

"Kyle and I were ambushed earlier. He was nabbed, so I was running back to town when I heard gunshots. I ran over to see if anyone needed help. That's when I saw you through the window. When I heard you hollering at the men, I crawled in through an open window and waited for you to make your move. You did good, Dalilah. Real good!"

"Oh, my God, Dad. Uncle Kyle is in that crate, and he doesn't have a breathing tube. And Brad has been shot!"

CHAPTER 56

DALILAH LIFTED BRAD'S neck to clear his airway, while Ray looked for a pry bar. He found a hammer and beat on the wood to create an air hole. He removed a portion of the lid and saw the green cadaver sealant. "What the hell is this?"

"It's what they use to send cadavers by freighter. Uncle Kyle is under that."

Ray dug through the formaldehyde until he felt Kyle's body. He lifted Kyle's head and cleared the gel from his mouth. He was barely breathing, and his face was swollen. Ray removed him from the crate and placed him on the floor. "Kyle, it's Ray. I've got you, my friend. You'll be okay now."

Kyle mumbled something, and Ray saw a smile. He was obviously still under the effects of some kind of narcotic.

"He may have been drugged. We've got to get the antidote. How's Brad?"

"He's still breathing, but he's lost a lot of blood. He saved my life, Dad. He took a bullet for me."

"All the radios and phones are jammed."

"No, wait. I saw Gregori using his cell phone earlier. Maybe one of the other men has a phone."

Dalilah found a cell phone on the belt of the man she had killed. She dialed 9-1-1. "It's working."

"Carteret County Emergency Services. Is this an emergency?"

"Yes, this is an emergency. My name is Dalilah Smith. I need to make contact with Special Agent Rickard of the Federal Task Force. Russians here. Two officers down. Pier 18 warehouse. Port Terminal Road. One gunshot and one assault. We need EMS now!"

Ray and Dalilah looked at each other as they knelt beside their friends. It would take the ambulance a few minutes to arrive. Even though Kyle and Brad were stable for now, some Reiki energy would ensure their recovery.

CHAPTER 57

LIZA FELT HERSELF floating in some sort of gel. She was very cold and she had a terrible headache. She tried to move her hands, but they were bound with cord. She opened her eyes and saw a cloudy greenish glow. Her eyes burned so she closed them quickly. Liza felt the breathing tube in her mouth. The tape holding the tube pinched her face. She had no frame of reference as to what she was in other than JELL-O. She wondered how long she had been inside this mess. The last thing she remembered was struggling with some of Gregori's men.

Liza's thoughts rambled between reality and hallucination. Her thoughts were random at best despite her desperate attempts to concentrate. *Where am I? How long have I been here? How long will it be until I see someone? Is that you, Kyle?*

Surely this is not the way I am going to die? Kyle, where are you? Dalilah?

Liza found herself in a series of mental loops until a jarring movement brought her back to reality. *I must still be alive or I wouldn't have felt that.* Then she felt a choppy motion, like being on a boat. Liza concentrated. She had a strong feeling something was about to happen, but her consciousness faded.

***

Gregori's men made their final adjustments to the rubber raft at the edge of the surf. The men had brought Liza and Sarah's crates back to the cabin where they loaded them onto the raft. The men pulled away as Gregori watched the raft disappear into the night. The outboard motor could be heard as it churned away at the choppy surf. Gregori had given them specific orders, times and locations. It was imperative that the orders be followed exactly for the operation to work as Gregori had so skillfully planned.

He was sending two men out to rendezvous with the Russian freighter en route to Morehead City. He had arranged for the diamond shipment that normally went to Joseph to be dropped five miles from shore, two miles away from the normal delivery site.

Joseph's activities had been of interest to Gregori for some time. Gregori's crime syndicate had arranged for the delivery of the diamonds from northern Russia. The delivery method had worked so well that Gregori's group wanted to use the same system to transport heroin. None of Joseph's operatives had ever been arrested. None of his shipments had ever been confiscated. The system was foolproof.

Gregori knew the jeweler was really an intelligence agent working for various Middle-Eastern countries. The jewelry store was a front not only to accumulate funding for secret operations, but also to line the pockets of the intelligence agency's senior partners. The support Joseph received from various clients was incredible. The network stretched around the world.

Gregori was sure he had met Joseph at least once during his tenure as a career spy. He knew Joseph was a formidable opponent and that he would have to be careful since Joseph was so well connected. Gregori's goal was to do this last job, make tons of money and slip into obscurity. This night would be the culmination of his life's work.

Gregori walked back to the cabin and waited patiently for the two men. They would be en route to the cabin after having dispatched Dalilah and her boyfriend. Gregori took off his shoes to feel the sand on his feet. He pined for a vacation and a fine woman. He had grown fond of Liza, but he knew that their worlds could never be in harmony. After all, he was her kidnapper. He pondered all the failed relationships that had passed through his life like sacrificial fodder. Duty first. What nonsense!

His allegiance was to his country and then to his bosses. Boss was a term he used loosely. He knew what they really were. They were thugs in suits—upperclass thieves and power-mongers. Good choices during the Soviet breakup had given them positions in the various security agencies. Now they wielded the power in illegal activities all over the world, and Gregori was their front man. His reputation haunted him everywhere he went—the mechanic—the guy who fixed everything and got the job done no matter what. He caught himself feeling miserable. He took a deep breath and wiggled his toes in the sand.

Gregori looked at his cell phone to make sure he hadn't missed a call. He had instructed the men to notify him when they left the warehouse. The problem with his inept helpers stemmed from their family ties with the bosses. Sometimes the crime lords demanded that a nephew, cousin or other family acquaintance be given an opportunity to gain business experience. More often than not, none of the family members had any covert or military training. They knew nothing of discipline or work ethics. Since their relatives were in charge, they felt superior, making them dangerous to the mission and to everyone around them.

Gregori had inherited three such buffoons on this trip. Vladimir was one of them. The other two were still at the warehouse. It was a simple task. Kill the girl and the boyfriend; stuff them in a cadaver crate; return to the cabin. If they had been real intelligence operatives, Gregori would have been worried because of the late hour. With these two amateurs, he allowed extra time. Who knows, they might have stopped for pizza. So he waited. He was a patient man.

Gregori felt a vibration on his hip. He checked his cell phone and read the text message from his men on the raft. The Russian freighter had been spotted, and the raft was maneuvering into position to intercept.

***

A spotlight flashed the signal from the top deck of the ship. Using night vision binoculars, Gregori's men spotted two crates being dumped into the ocean off the ship's stern. It took them no time to reach the two containers. One man pulled a crate along the port side of the raft and pried it open. He reached into the cadaver and removed ten clear bags of brown, crusty Russian diamonds.

After searching for additional bags, he cut loose the flotation material and placed it in the raft. The crate and cadaver sank quickly. He then made quick work of the second crate. He removed another ten bags of Russian diamonds and placed the flotation cushions into the raft.

The crate bobbed momentarily, then sank under the waves. The two Russians looked at the bags of diamonds sitting on the bottom of the raft. If it were not for Gregori's reputation and their fear of retaliation, they might have stolen the diamonds. Twenty million dollars was tempting. So close, yet so far.

The older man proved to be the cautious one. He suggested that they do as Gregori had said. Otherwise, they would never have peace in their lives, always looking over their shoulders, always wondering if Gregori knew where they were hiding.

He was too old to live that way. The other Russian laughed and agreed. At least it was exciting, even for a fleeting moment, to think about such an enterprise.

Both men grabbed the flotation material and attached it to the crates holding Liza and Sarah. After double-checking their work, they left to intercept the freighter again. The Russian freighter had slowed its speed as it approached the port area, allowing the raft to catch up quickly. Gregori's man steered the raft into the wake of the large ship, about three hundred yards beyond the stern.

The other man looked through his night vision binoculars for the usual signal designated for Joseph. They were still in international waters about three miles from the shore. Once Gregori's man saw the flashing signal, he pushed both crates from the raft into the water. Gregori had given special instructions that the crates were to float. He didn't want the women drowned.

Mission accomplished, the raft headed back to the cabin. The older man sent a text message to Gregori—Cargo received. Cargo delivered.

CHAPTER 58

RAY GENTLY ROLLED Kyle on his side as Dalilah placed cardboard underneath to insulate his body against the cold concrete. They moved Brad beside Kyle and did the same for him. Dalilah found a crushed box and used it as a pillow for Brad's head.

Ray used a small wooden pole and traced a circle on the floor around Kyle and Brad. This was the ceremonial Sacred Circle used to ritualize and sanctify an area. Ray started in the East and drew the circle in a clockwise direction. The circle was completed when he returned to the East.

Ray sat inside the Sacred Circle in a half-lotus position by Kyle's side, while Dalilah sat in a full-lotus meditative position next to Brad. Ray and Dalilah faced each other, with the two men between them. With the ambulance a few minutes away, they used the time to infuse the wounded men with Reiki energy.

Dalilah and her dad were students of many ancient healing methods. They used a familiar Reiki visualization of a white mist gathering at the base of the spine or root chakra. In this power center located in the perineum, the dragon or serpent sleeps until it is summoned to perform its magical duties. They continued this breathing rhythm as the life-force energy grew stronger.

On the fifth breath, they visualized the mist turning violet and rising up the spinal column as the serpent uncoiled, activating the Kundalini energy. They exhaled the dragon chi breath in a deep, resonant tone. Now Kyle and Brad were covered with a violet mist. The mist did not evaporate as it encircled their bodies. It clung to their auric outline like a soap bubble surrounding their bodies. Their injuries made their energy fields very weak. Ray and Dalilah then moved their hands in concentric counterclockwise circles above Brad and Kyle's bodies while saying, "Cho Ku Rei. Cho Ku Rei. Cho Ku Rei." The chant literally meant, "By Divine Decree. Put the Power here."

Then they used the second power symbol, the Master symbol. Drawing the Tibetan symbol in the air above the bodies, they repeated in unison, "Dai ko mio. Dai ko mio. Dai ko mio." The warehouse echoed with the ancient chant.

The final symbol was a repetition of the first. It completed the trinity of the healing power. They moved their hands in a circle and repeated, "Cho Ku Rei. Cho Ku Rei. Cho Ku Rei."

Dalilah and Ray took several deep breaths and continued to exhale the dragon breath. The energy encapsulated Brad and Kyle, then turned the violet mist into a glowing sphere of golden-blue light.

CHAPTER 59

DALILAH AND HER dad made final preparations for the Tibetan Medicine Buddha chant. This chant would bring in the healing energy of the Lapis Blue Medicine Buddha.

Dalilah remembered how she had laughed the first time her dad had told her about the Medicine Buddha. He had said to think of him as a Smurf Buddha because he was totally blue. In Tibetan Buddhism, there were five main colors of significance—yellow for earth, white for wind, red for fire, green for water and blue for space, ethers or the heavens. Her dad had also said to be respectful of the Medicine Buddha because when the chant was said in earnest, it would heal with incredible power.

Dalilah made eye contact with her dad as he nodded. They chanted in unison in a deep, low tone. "Tayatha Om Bekhaze Bekhaze Maha Bekhaze Bekhaze Raja Samugate Soha. Tayatha Om Bekhaze Bekhaze Maha Bekhaze Bekhaze Raja Samugate Soha . . . "

They continued with total focus, repeating the chant seven times. Then something happened that Dalilah had never seen before. Her dad had once told her that the power of the Medicine Buddha chant reached into the past and future, spanning all time. It invoked the energies of the Buddha, all Reiki Masters, Tibetan priests and anyone else who shared the wisdom of the Medicine Buddha. It pierced the veils of consciousness, allowing the healing love to travel to any part of the universe.

Dalilah heard the droning of the Medicine Buddha chant. She was not chanting; neither was her dad. The golden-blue bubble they had placed around Kyle and Brad slowly transformed into a bluish hue. The sound of the chant continued as Dalilah absorbed its wonderful energy. She felt as if she were floating in the air. As she opened her eyes again, the energy bubble surrounding Kyle and Brad had reached the full spectrum of its radiance—a sparkling royal blue. The color rivaled that of the deepest lapis lazuli stone.

As she looked around the room, she saw Tibetan monks floating around the Sacred Circle. She looked at her dad as he smiled and repeated the chant with his Spirit partners. Then a bright light shone from above as if the sun itself were in the room. The light was brilliant, yet it didn't hurt Dalilah's eyes. She looked at her hands. They glowed an iridescent white mixed with royal blue. Intuitively, she knew to face her palms toward Brad.

When she turned her hands toward Brad, the energy came out of her palms like a sunbeam, illuminating Brad's entire body. Shards of light moved in and out of his physical body and energy field. Brad's body glowed. Then Dalilah heard a voice in her head . . . *Your love has healed him. Your love has healed him. Your love has healed him.*

Dalilah was not sure who was talking, but she knew this was not her imagination. She felt energized. She felt the love she had for Brad and the love he had for her. She felt true love—the kind of love that created the universe and sustained it with infinite compassion every second of every day. She felt the unconditional love God had for everyone and everything. She was experiencing the oneness her dad had talked about. *We are one with everyone and everything in the universe.*

All along, this feeling had been nestled in her heart. It had been blocked by so much unfinished emotional baggage. Now she understood. Her dad had told her she would have to learn this on her own. He could show her the way, but the journey was up to her. God was everywhere, in everyone and in everything. God was love. Where God was, love was. Even in this dusty, dirty warehouse, love existed.

She looked at her dad and knew he was feeling the oneness. He had shared his knowledge long ago. But who has time to listen to their parents? He was right. *I had to take the journey myself.*

Just as Dalilah was getting lost in the increasing presence of the power of love, Brad coughed. She looked at his body and saw him move. He was alive and conscious. Dalilah started to get up before she remembered she had to say thank you to her Spirit helpers. Dalilah heard her dad reminding her to be thankful for all gifts, especially those from Spirit. Too often, we humans receive wonderful gifts from heaven, but we fail to acknowledge them with a simple thank you.

The droning of the Medicine Buddha chant subsided as the energy bubble around Kyle and Brad dissipated. Dalilah felt extreme heat around her body. Her dad had begun a Tibetan chant for thanking the Spirit helpers as he brought the healing ceremony to an end.

When he neared the end of the chant, he glanced at Dalilah. She knew the ceremony had to end in an exalted state, just as it had begun. This allowed the energy to be sealed into Brad and Kyle's bodies. Dalilah and Ray clapped their hands together, shouting, "*Pau.*" This was an ending used in Huna, a shamanic system of ancient Hawaiian culture. The word simply meant "it's over."

Dalilah moved closer to Brad. His eyes opened. She rubbed his face and said playfully, "Well, marine, are you going to get up sometime soon?"

Brad smiled. "Yeah, if you can get this pickup truck off my chest. It feels like somebody pumped air into me."

Dalilah knew right away he had a punctured lung, so she turned him on his side to alleviate the pain. She had a good feeling about Brad's recovery. She would not mention the Medicine Buddha ceremony to him unless he asked. Dalilah could hear the sirens. She looked over, and Uncle Kyle smiled at her.

"Good job, kid. I saw you work your magic. You are your dad's daughter. Thank God."

"I'm so glad you're feeling better, Uncle Kyle. You had us worried."

"Have you heard anything about Liza?"

"No. But we'll find her."

Two teams of paramedics entered the warehouse. Kyle smiled as Ray helped him onto the stretcher. Ray told the paramedics Kyle had been exposed to Fentanyl. They started an IV immediately and administered a saline solution.

Dalilah held Brad's hand as the gurney was rolled to the ambulance. A paramedic had inserted a chest tube to relieve the pressure, and Brad was breathing more easily. With an oxygen mask over his mouth, he couldn't speak. Dalilah said, "I love you."

Brad used eyelash Morse cord and blinked three times to signal his love for her. Ray and Dalilah embraced each other as they watched the ambulances drive away.

"You did a great job, sweetheart."

"Thanks, Dad. That was incredible."

"We make a great team, don't we? Now, let's find Liza and this Gregori fellow. We have some unfinished business."

CHAPTER 60

A FTER RECEIVING THE signal from the freighter, Joseph engaged the engines and slowly made his way to the crates. He never saw the Russians in the raft. Neither did he suspect anything out of the ordinary. The Russian cargo ship had flashed the signal as it always did, and Joseph had spotted the crates. It seemed to be a routine pick-up.

As he moved closer, Joseph slowed the engines as Ben positioned himself on the platform at the stern of the yacht. This shipment called for three containers, but there were only two. Ben used the portable spotlight to search for the other crate while Joseph used the deck searchlight to scan the ocean's surface. As they got closer, Joseph noticed a white tube extending out of each crate. He thought this to be highly unusual, and he did not like the feeling.

Ben gaffed the first crate and pulled it in. He lifted the crate partially onto the platform. The waves had grown larger, and he found it difficult to maintain his balance. Joseph immediately looked over the box to ensure that it was not rigged with explosives. He told Ben to step back. He would open the first crate himself.

Joseph pried off the lid gently and slowly. After lifting the wood a few inches, he searched the underside for any electronic parts or wiring that would indicate a bomb. After searching the entire lid, he was satisfied everything was kosher. Ben stepped up and they lifted the top off. Everything looked normal. The green cadaver sealant and the outline of a human body looked just like the other ones from the previous excursion.

Ben reached into the cold gel and searched for the stitches on the chest of the cadaver. He had forgotten just how cold it was. He felt a hand grab his. Ben jumped back and screamed. Joseph ran to his side.

"What is it, Ben?"

"It grab-b-bed m-m-me-eee!" Ben stuttered.

"That's impossible, son. They're dead."

"No. I know something grabbed my hand and squeezed it."

Joseph carefully inspected the cadaver. Even with the waves lapping against the hull of the yacht, he thought he heard someone mumbling. He placed his ear closer to the white tube. He heard someone groaning. The tube was a breathing tube.

Joseph ripped through the cadaver gel to expose a woman's face. He removed the tape from around her mouth and pulled out the tube. The woman coughed and gagged as Joseph dug out more of the green gel. Ben clawed into the torso area as he threw the gel into the ocean.

The woman groaned and coughed as she tried to breathe. After removing most of the sealant, Joseph and Ben carried her to the deck above the platform. Joseph grabbed a blanket from the port side storage bin and covered her. She was naked, shivering and blue. The woman was saying something, but it was hard for them to hear her. Her voice was very weak.

"Dali . . . Da . . . Dalilah."

"Did she say Dalilah?"

"I don't know, son. Keep her covered and give her some water. I'll go for the other crate. It may have another live person."

Liza lay in the blanket and mumbled. Her body shivered uncontrollably, almost like a seizure. Ben tried to keep her covered, but the roll of the yacht was making it difficult. Ben listened as Liza spoke softly, "Kyle. Kyle . . . "

Joseph used the gaff to reach for the other crate. Twice he tried to bring it in. A large wave moved it closer. He reached out and snagged a piece of the flotation material. Part of the rope was cut as an entire side of flotation ballast separated from the container. Joseph pulled hard with the gaff. Seawater covered the lid and the white tube was submerged several times.

The waves became troublesome as Joseph struggled to save the box. With one last hard tug, he brought the crate close enough to secure it to the rear landing at water level. He pried open the lid and frantically dug through the gel to locate the person's face. He lifted with all his might, but the sealant was too thick. He would have to remove more of it to bring the body out of the crate.

Joseph shouted, "I'm going to get you out. Hold on."

He feared the person inside might be in serious trouble since the breathing tube had gone under the water. Joseph continued to shovel the cadaver gel out with his hands. After removing a sufficient amount, he cleared away the victim's face.

Joseph was mortified. He froze. Everything went quiet in his mind. He could hear his heartbeat and his own shallow breathing. What seemed like an eternity was only a few seconds. Then he screamed, "Sarah! Sarah! Sarah!"

Ben heard his father shout his mother's name. He ran to his side and saw his mother, still and not breathing. The tube had come away from her mouth, and her lips were blue.

"Mom! Mom! No! Mom, come back! Come back to us!"

Ben and Joseph reached into the crate as a rogue wave washed it into the Atlantic Ocean. The men were no match for the strength of the sea, and Sarah slipped from their hands. Without hesitation, Ben jumped into the water to rescue his mother. As he hit the water, Joseph hollered, "No, Ben! No!"

Joseph grabbed the spotlight and illuminated the dark water, hoping Ben could use it to locate Sarah. Ben was an excellent swimmer. He had strong shoulders, strong legs and a lanky frame. A perfect swimmer.

Panic set in as Joseph felt hopeless. Then the surface erupted with a deep, moaning breath. He shined the spotlight and found Ben fifty feet off the port stern. Another figure floated next to him.

Joseph threw out a lifeline. Ben placed the flotation ring around his mother as Joseph pulled both of them in. Ben was exhausted and barely able to lift himself out of the water. Joseph brought his wife onto the rear platform and then pulled his son out of the ocean. After Ben regained his strength, father and son lifted Sarah to the main deck. She was not breathing.

Joseph's emotions subsided and his training kicked in. He reverted to a highly skilled operative able to overcome any obstacle. He told Ben to get the portable defibrillator next to the first aid kit. Then he began CPR.

Joseph stopped CPR when Ben returned. He activated the battery pack and placed the electrodes onto Sarah's chest and rib cage. In ten seconds, the system was ready to send fifty thousand volts through Sarah's lifeless body. Joseph shouted, "Stand back."

Sarah shivered and jumped as the electrical current reeled through her body. Joseph checked for a pulse. There was none. He reset the machine, and again Sarah's body convulsed wildly. Her pulse was weak, but there was a pulse. She coughed. He turned her onto her side as seawater and foam poured from her lungs. Joseph rubbed her face as Ben placed a blanket over her naked body. She was unconscious. Alive, but unconscious.

Joseph's mind exploded with scenarios. *How did this happen?* They made their way back to the marina at full speed. He picked up his radio and spoke with his security team.

"Charlie One. Charlie One. 10-33. EMS two victims in shock. We are secure."

"Charlie One copy. EMS is being dispatched. Two victims in shock. Marina is secure. Be advised we are under SATCOM and scrambled. Receiving electronic interference. No other activity."

The security protocols established by Joseph were activated. A 10-33 code meant an emergency, so backup security teams were immediately placed on stand-by. Joseph couldn't rule out being monitored so he selected his language carefully.

Joseph radioed back to the security team. "Charlie One. Send Alpha team, COM center. Bravo, home. Sarah is not there. I have her here. Charlie team with me to the hospital."

Charlie One responded, "10-4. Say again. Sarah is with you?"

"That's affirmative. She's one of the victims."

"10-4. EMS has arrived and standing by."

Joseph suspected his team leader was now very confused. Even so, he knew his orders would be followed without question. The most important thing was the family was with him and safe.

Joseph saw the harbor lights as he slowed but continued well above the legal approaching speed. He did not send a message to the harbormaster to declare an emergency. He thought this situation should be kept quiet. The flashing lights of the ambulance lit up the marina. He looked back at Ben, who held his mother in his lap, crying and praying.

I've grown sloppy and let myself be set up. I'm a fool to be caught unaware. He would find out who did this. Nobody fucked with his family! No one. Someone would die a prolonged, painful death.

CHAPTER 61

A SEA OF task force members combed every inch of the warehouse collecting evidence. The bodies of the Russians had been tagged and bagged. Their chalk lines remained for reference.

Dalilah and Ray completed their preliminary debriefing. Special Agent Rickard gave them the next steps in the process since they were technically under his supervision.

"Do we know where Gregori is?" Ray asked.

"No, my men haven't located him yet. He's still in the city. I'm sure of that. He's here to pick up something."

"Who is Gregori?" Dalilah asked.

"Well," Rickard said, "the short answer is that he's an international terrorist, assassin and drug runner. The long answer is that he's an ex-KGB agent who now uses his exceptional skills in the service of the highest bidder. And usually the highest bidder is involved with international criminal enterprises. You name it, and I imagine Gregori did it."

"How do you know so much about him?" Ray asked.

Rickard hesitated. "He killed some friends of mine in Europe. We were on a stakeout, watching some Russian drug lords, when things went south. There was an explosion. Everybody except me was killed. I later found out through some CIA sources that Gregori masterminded the hit. He was paid handsomely for his efforts. Due to the impact of the deaths, all investigations concerning Russian drug lords came to a halt. Gregori's actions essentially shut down all drug investigations with INTERPOL, the German Secret Police and other European intelligence agencies. He had quite a reputation after that event. Because of that, he can name his price for any job. He is the highest-paid troubleshooter in the world."

Ray shook his head. "Dalilah, you surely know how to pick a case, don't you?"

"Dad, I had no idea. I usually find information others can't. A one-day job, two at the most. I send in the information. I get paid."

"I know, sweetheart. Believe me, this is not your fault. You just got caught in the middle. They used your expertise to locate the leaks in their operation. They wanted to know just how secure they were. I don't know what you did or found out, but evidently they weren't as invisible as they thought. But don't worry. We will rectify this situation."

Rickard agreed. "You can bet Gregori won't snake his way out of this one."

Rickard's cell phone rang. He nodded as he mumbled into the phone.

"How is it that your phone is working?" Ray asked

"During the search of the warehouse we found an electronic jamming device taped to a steel beam. That's why the radios went out. It knocked out every electronic signal within a mile. I've got to get back to the command center now. I have a fax coming in. Do you two need a ride?"

"No," Dalilah said, "we can use Sergeant Lewis' patrol vehicle."

Rickard left the warehouse, leaving Ray and Dalilah to discuss their next move.

"Okay, Dad, new game plan. Any ideas?"

"Do you remember Rickard saying that Gregori was here to pick up something?"

"Yes, I do."

"Well, what do you suppose that is?"

"It's got to be drugs. Didn't Rickard say he was a drug runner and that he worked for the Russian drug lords?"

"Yes, he did. We're in a port. It has to be a cargo ship. Why else would he be in a port city?"

"Plus it's a smaller port city. Not like Philadelphia or Wilmington. Out of the way, yet large enough to handle commercial freighters."

"Okay. Let's have a look at the papers you found on the dead guys. That may give us something to go on."

CHAPTER 62

DALILAH EMPTIED HER pockets. She hadn't given the CSI personnel any of the papers she'd removed from the Russians. Their pockets had been full of scrap paper, notes and receipts. They were surely amateurs to keep so much information on them, or perhaps they were arrogant enough to think they wouldn't be caught.

Ray and Dalilah searched through the papers, many of them wet with blood. Most were fast-food and convenience store receipts from Morehead City and Atlantic Beach. Then Dalilah opened a folded piece of paper.

"Dad, I think I have an address. It's got to be their hideout."

Ray looked at the paper, which looked like a scrap from a grocery bag. "Well, it has a street number. Maybe they were amateurs, and they really had no worries. Gregori boosted their confidence. This will work for us."

"Brad has a street guide in his patrol car. Maybe we can verify the address or at least the street name."

They went to the SUV. Dalilah found a guide with all the streets in Carteret County and a special section for Morehead City. When she found the street, she shouted, "We've got them!"

Dalilah cranked up the SUV and they headed south to Atlantic Beach, across the causeway from Morehead City. The address was 1218 West Ocean Ridge Drive near the west end of Atlantic Beach.

"Dalilah, I am so proud of you and the way you handle yourself. You have turned into quite a woman. Not only professionally, but also spiritually. I couldn't have done that ceremony without you. You've certainly increased your healing skills."

"Thanks, Dad. I'm just doing what you taught me. Plus, you know, I have Mom's strength, too."

"Yes, you do."

They were close to the address. Maybe this was the house the Russians had rented, and maybe this was where they had taken Liza. Dalilah saw the address on the mailbox. Lights were on in the house, and a van was in the driveway. They were on a secluded part of the beach that had few houses. She drove past the driveway and cut her lights. She clicked on the switch that killed the taillights. Hopefully, the Russians were sloppy in all aspects of their mission and wouldn't notice a car driving by.

Dalilah and Ray left the Trailblazer and gently closed its doors. With the strong sound of the surf, their movements would be unheard. Dalilah checked all her gear again. Ray picked up the Maglite, and they moved slowly toward the bungalow.

The sand dunes gave the pair excellent cover as they eased to the side of the house to look in one of the larger windows. Through her binoculars, Dalilah saw three men. One of them was Gregori. They were huddled around a table looking at something.

Dalilah handed the binoculars to her dad, but Ray was unable to tell what held the men's attention. "It looks like some sort of brown material, but I can't make it out. It could be drugs, probably heroin."

They moved in closer, hoping to find Liza inside. As they proceeded, Dalilah scoured the ground, looking for trip wires or flares that might signal their approach. Apparently the Russians were not into security. They really hadn't allowed for the possibility they might be caught.

Ray and Dalilah squatted in front of a window. The rough surf drowned out most of what was being said. The only sound they heard clearly was laughter. When they did hear some words, they were in Russian.

Ray motioned that he was going to circle the house to search for Liza. Dalilah stayed by the window, hoping the men would say something in English.

Ray moved with as much stealth as Dalilah, even though he was twenty-five years her senior. He did a full reconnaissance around the house and returned within a few minutes. He pointed to the dunes, and he and Dalilah moved to better cover.

"I didn't see any crates inside the house, and I looked in the van. Nothing. Liza is not here."

"Where could she be, Dad? I saw them take her out with the other crate."

"I don't know, sweetheart. Why don't you do a psychic search?"

"Okay. I'll try."

"They're drinking Vodka inside. They won't be a problem. I'm going to the car and radio the command center. Wait 'til I get back, and I'll keep watch."

CHAPTER 63

RAY RETURNED QUICKLY. "The cavalry is on the way. Okay, sweetheart, do your thing."

Dalilah, despite the tremendous stress, allowed herself to be quiet inside. She centered herself, thinking of the slow-moving river as it emptied into the placid lake. She envisioned herself on a deck having a glass of tea with Liza.

Once she felt calm, she imagined Liza's face. She whispered her name in her mind. Liza. Liza. Liza. Where are you? Are you all right? I need a picture of your surroundings.

Dalilah moved into a deep state of meditation on the theta level. With her eyes closed, her higher self searched for any clues within the universal web of life. Dalilah believed everything was connected to everything else. She was counting on her spiritual training to guide her. She knew she could access information leading to Liza's whereabouts.

Dalilah entered a dream state of reality called the one-percent shaman. This technique of spiritual journeying ensured Dalilah could control her progress and make changes in her meditation as the situation warranted. By releasing all fears and preconceptions, she would allow ninety-nine percent of her energy field to be pure, flowing spirit. One percent of her energy would retain her own psyche. She decided to call upon her Spirit helper the Eagle.

The Spirit Eagle arrived quickly in her mind. She asked the eagle to search for any imprint of Liza's energy field. Dalilah imagined riding on the eagle's back and flying over the ocean and along Atlantic Beach and Morehead City. Near the interior of the city, she spotted a bright glow. The eagle flew toward the light and hovered over the area. Dalilah saw a helicopter landing pad and a large red cross on the roof. It looked like a hospital.

Dalilah asked her helper how this could be Liza's location. She quickly disregarded the doubting thought and accepted the vision as it was given. They continued to hover, and she felt a strong presence of Liza's energy. Liza was somehow in the hospital, alive and recovering strength as indicated by her increasing light. This was a great sign.

The eagle flew back to the dune as Dalilah imagined sliding down from its back. She thanked the Spirit Eagle for its help as it flew off into the night sky. She took a deep breath and moved her fingers and wiggled her toes. She felt her physical body as she became fully conscious and aware of her surroundings. She opened her eyes and saw her dad.

"Dad, how long was I out?"

"About fifteen minutes. I know it seemed longer."

"I found Liza. She's in the hospital."

"But how? Never mind. We must trust the vision. We must have faith that we have the power to dream."

"Yes, she's in the hospital, and she's okay. I felt her getting stronger."

"Great news. Good job, sweetheart. And just in time."

Ray pointed toward the street as Dalilah grabbed the binoculars. She saw a black van creeping down the road. Then a flash of metal and figures running in the dark. The SWAT team surrounded the building. Rickard used a bullhorn to order the men out of the house.

The entire house went dark. The Russians had cut off the lights. After a few seconds, an explosion shattered the night. The flash ruined everyone's night vision. Shots were fired. Everyone took cover as the shots continued.

Dalilah and Ray heard a motor being started. Dalilah crawled to another dune and spotted someone on a rubber raft headed out to sea. He was too far away to identify.

She turned her attention back to the house where two men ran out toward the van. SWAT officers intercepted them, and a volley of gunfire erupted. The men were caught in a crossfire and didn't stand a chance. A small fire blazed inside the bungalow, lighting the driveway. Two more Russians lay dead.

CHAPTER 64

KYLE OPENED HIS eyes and felt disoriented. He must have dozed off in the ambulance. The effects of the Fentanyl still impaired his sensory awareness. He remembered lots of blue light from the healing ceremony. He did feel better, and he knew he was going to live. Kyle could see a blue curtain surrounding his bed, so he surmised he was in the emergency room. He attempted to get up, but he felt as if he weighed a ton. He decided just to be still. He lay in bed and tried some deep breathing.

Now was a good time to try that meditation stuff Ray and Dalilah had preached at him for years. After what he had just witnessed, he was inclined to be a real believer. Whatever they did, it worked, and he was the better for it. He decided to give it a try. Kyle relaxed and spoke to his body.

Heal yourself. Whatever the problem is, just heal. I have to be well. I must find Liza. Liza is alive and well. As Kyle repeated his inner mantras, he heard someone talking on the other side of the blue curtain.

"We don't know who she is," a nurse said. "EMS brought her in. She seems to be suffering from the same ailment as the other woman brought in at the same time, disorientation and shallow breathing. The other woman is Sarah Davidson. Her husband is with her. He told me he found them in some crates. Kidnap victims or something. There isn't much to go on."

"Odd that we have three victims with similar symptoms," the attending physician said. "Nothing life threatening, though. Monitor their respiratory rates and continue the IV until we can get the lab work back."

"Yes, doctor. I'll inform the nursing staff."

Kyle strained to hear more. He was able to comprehend only part of the doctor's conversation. It sounded as if two other people were in the same medical crisis as he. If he could get someone's attention, he could explain that it was probably Fentanyl poisoning.

***

A nurse entered the room next to Kyle's and checked the vitals of the Jane Doe. The patient was in her mid-fifties and quite attractive. Her hair was full of a greenish gel and had the odor of formaldehyde. Since the nurse wasn't sure what it was, she used an antibiotic scrub to clean her face and body. She stopped when she heard a commotion in the room across the hall.

***

Joseph and Ben were by Sarah's bedside. Ben was obviously still upset. "Mom, it's me, Ben. Mom, you're all right. You're in the hospital. Can you hear me, Mom?"

Her eyes were partly open, but she was unresponsive. At least she was breathing better now. Joseph had ridden in the ambulance with Sarah when she regained partial consciousness.

"Papa, look! She's crying. She's okay. She heard us."

"Sarah! I'm so sorry, Sarah! Forgive me, please. Everybody is all right, Sarah. Ben is fine. You'll be okay. You're in the hospital, and you'll make it. Just rest. We're here."

Ben held his mother's hand and wept by her bedside. Joseph brushed the hair from her face. She was still covered in the green gelatin. Joseph felt the rage building inside, but he knew he had to be calm. An enemy was close by, and he had to protect his family. He touched Ben's head and said, "Everything is fine, my son. We'll be all right. I'll make sure of that."

***

Rickard rushed into the emergency room with several agents behind him. "Where are Sergeants Steed and Lewis?" he shouted. "I'm Special Agent

Rickard. Homeland Security Task Force. They're my men."

The emergency room nurse explained that Sergeant Lewis was in surgery. She then guided Rickard to Steed's bed.

CHAPTER 65

"THANK GOD, SOMEBODY'S here," Steed said, seeing Rickard enter.

"Sergeant Steed, are you all right? It looks like they worked you over."

"Yeah, I'm fine. I think they used the Fentanyl on me. Ray and Dalilah saved my life."

"Yeah, those two don't mess around, do they? Well, we just raided Gregori's hideout. No sign of him."

"Did you find Liza?"

"Uh, no. We didn't find anyone else. The house exploded as the SWAT team was about to enter. Two Russians tried to shoot their way out, but they lost."

Kyle felt a heaviness on his shoulders. *Where is Liza?* All he could think about was the house exploding with Liza inside. *It's too late. She's gone.*

Rickard shouted for the doctor. "Hey, doc. My man needs the antidote for Fentanyl poisoning. Here's the CDC toxin report. It has all the information you'll need."

Naloxene from the hospital pharmacy had been ordered by the doctor. The hospital staff accelerated into high gear to counteract the poisoning effects of the Fentanyl.

***

Joseph overheard the Special Agent talking about Gregori. He knew exactly who Gregori was. He had heard of him among the intelligence field officers. But why has he done this to me? I've never crossed this man. But now, for whatever reason, we are enemies. Justice will be swift and final. An eye for an eye! Joseph grabbed his shirt and tore it.

CHAPTER 66

THE NURSE ADMINISTERED the first dose of the Naloxene to Kyle. She advised him to rest, assuring him that he would feel much better in a few minutes. "I'll be back soon to check on you, Sergeant Steed."

The nurse grabbed another vial of the antidote and rushed into Sarah's room. She injected the medicine into the IV tube and looked at Ben. "Your mother is going to be better now. Don't worry. I heard your dad say that you saved her from drowning."

***

Ben looked up at her and just barely smiled. He placed his forehead back on his mother's hand and continued his prayers. Joseph touched his son's head and left the room. He instructed two of his security officers at the hospital to stay at the entrance to guard Sarah and Ben. Then Joseph left with his other security team members.

***

The nurse made her way to Jane Doe's room. The patient was barely alert. The nurse spoke to her and told her she would feel better in no time. She didn't act like she heard anything. The nurse spoke a little louder. "This is the antidote. You'll be all right, dear. Just rest."

***

Special Agent Rickard stepped into Kyle's room. "I'm leaving an officer here until you feel better. Let us know if you remember anything about Gregori?"

Kyle shook his head. The nurse entered and checked his IV. His eyes were swollen, but they burned with a mission. His mind was reeling with dozens of scenarios. Thoughts of Liza consumed his every breath. He laid his head back on the pillow. "Liza. I'll find you," he whispered.

CHAPTER 67

LIZA WAS BEGINNING to feel human again. Her vision cleared, and she was able to hear better after the nurse removed green gel from both ears. She felt tired and had a slight headache. She lay in bed thinking of Kyle. Dozing off, she whispered, "Kyle."

***

Kyle's body responded quickly to the antidote. He sat up in bed and tried to make sense of what had happened. To clear his head, Kyle did some deep breathing. All he could think about was Liza. His stomach churned; but in his head, he pictured Liza's bright eyes and smiling face. With a new burst of energy, he shouted to the shadow on the other side of the curtain, "Officer, any word on Liza or Gregori?"

***

Liza listened as her heart raced. Kyle's voice sounded so clear. So close. She spoke loudly. "Kyle. Where are you?"

The blue curtain pulled back, and Kyle's battered body revealed itself. "Liza, it's you! I was so afraid I'd lost you!"

They reached for each other's hands, but the beds were too far apart. Tears ran down their faces. Liza, in a trembling voice, said, "I knew you'd find me."

CHAPTER 68

DALILAH'S CELL PHONE vibrated on her hip. She grabbed it.

"Dalilah, this is Kyle. I have Liza. She's with me in the hospital."

"Oh, my God! Dad, Liza's in the hospital with Uncle Kyle. Uncle Kyle, how did she get there?"

"EMS brought her in with another woman. Both of them were covered in the green gel."

"How about Brad? Have you heard anything from his surgery?"

"Yeah, he's fine. As a matter of fact, he's supposed to join us in an hour. They're keeping us together for a debriefing. It seems no one knows what's going on, so they're keeping all of us together until somebody can figure it out."

"Okay, Uncle Kyle. We have a bead on Gregori. We think he's headed for a Russian freighter. We're on our way to the Coast Guard Station to get some help."

"All right. Be careful. Take care of your dad."

Ray turned into the Coast Guard Station at Fort Macon. Dalilah had called Lieutenant Roberts for assistance. He was waiting at the door as they exited their vehicle. Dalilah shook his hand.

"Well, Dalilah, I must say that it's a pleasure to see you again. I'm glad to hear Brad will be all right."

"Lieutenant Roberts, this is my dad, Ray Kim."

Ray and the lieutenant exchanged hand-shakes.

"Are you two ready?" Lieutenant Roberts said. "We have a cutter standing by."

"Yes, we are!" Dalilah said.

"Brad is a good friend of mine. We can't have people shooting our police officers and then hiding aboard foreign vessels." The lieutenant was shaking his head. "It might have been a safe haven years ago, but not since 9/11."

"We can't officially take any criminal investigative action in reference to the kidnapping. *Posse comitatus* prevents military forces from taking civilian police actions except in times of national emergency. We can, however, conduct port security inspections for weapons, narcotics and contraband. And if you, being part of a multi-jurisdictional task force, report to me the possibility of a terrorist on board, then we have a search to complete. And since this particular freighter did not adhere to the seventy-two-hour notification policy, we have all the legal justification we need. So, let's go hunting."

***

Ray and Dalilah could go on this mission because they were assigned to the federal task force and for suspect identification, should Gregori be stowed away. Roberts led them toward the dock where several large Coast Guard ships were moored. He pointed to the CGC Chilula, a 205-foot medium endurance cutter, which would do the job for their boarding inspection.

Dalilah and Ray went directly to the bridge with the lieutenant. The cutter slowly made its way out of port and waited in the shipping lane for the Russian freighter Nicholas III to get closer to port. The Coast Guard cutter maneuvered so as to block its path in preparation for boarding. As the cargo ship moved closer, the radioman announced, "This is the United States Coast Guard Cutter Chilula. Halt all engines and prepare to be boarded."

The ship did not respond and continued on a collision course. Roberts ordered the cutter to maneuver parallel to the freighter's direction. The machine gunner on the bow stood ready to issue a more impressive warning. As the freighter came closer, neither slowing nor attempting radio communications, Lieutenant Roberts shouted, "Chief Petty Officer Milam, how about welcoming them to the United States of America."

"Aye, Aye, Captain."

Milam racked back the slide on the fifty-caliber machine gun. A burst of rounds shot across the freighter's bow sent seawater erupting ten feet into the air. The tracer rounds, glowing red with white phosphorous tips, made an intermittent line of fire across the ocean waves. The noise was deafening and Dalilah covered her ears. The radio came alive in Russian and broken English. The Russian freighter slowed to a standstill.

Roberts ordered the cutter to maneuver alongside. Coast Guard sailors boarded the Russian freighter, armed with rifles and sidearms. The lieutenant followed his crew across the gangplank and was confronted by the Russian captain as he emerged from the bridge.

Roberts spoke sternly to him. "Have all your men line up on the top deck. I want a manifest to show your cargo and exact personnel count."

The captain of the Nicholas III provided Roberts with the manifest. The freighter was hauling agricultural products and machine parts, with a total manpower of one hundred twenty-two men. The ship originated from a small port city north of Moscow. Roberts ordered a contraband search for weapons and narcotics. All the freighter's sailors remained on deck as the search took place.

***

Meanwhile, Gregori was in the cargo hold, searching for the special crates that contained his precious narcotics. All he needed was the ten kilos to fulfill his delivery contract. He wanted time to find the additional ten kilos he had shipped for his personal business ventures. Gregori always had extra kilos sent so he could expand his personal drug business. Unknown to his boss, Ivan, he'd been doing that for years. And he had become a wealthy man in the process.

The cadaver crates had been placed in a special area so they could be unloaded and later retrieved by the forklift operator Gregori had hired. The crates were located. He dug into the cadavers and removed the brown-packaged blocks of pure Afghani heroin. The opium and heroin were supposedly of the purest quality in the world. And people were willing to pay for such quality. Gregori's personal customers were very wealthy and well known in America's social circles.

Gregori placed his shipments inside a large duffel bag. All he had to do now was to wait out the inspection and be on his way. Several of the sailors on board worked for his organization. All of them knew Gregori or at least his reputation. They were willing to assist him in trade for the luxuries and promotions he provided.

CHAPTER 69

DALILAH AND RAY heard the radio traffic between Lieutenant Roberts and one of his men. Some cargo crates had been demolished, and they were filled with dead bodies and green sealant.

Dalilah, Ray and the lieutenant went down to the cargo area. Three crates had been broken into. The cadavers were exposed, their chests ripped open. Dalilah knew why.

After a search of the ship failed to find Gregori, Roberts allowed the freighter to enter the port. The Coast Guard cutter returned to the station. Dalilah and Ray knew Gregori had been there. Somehow he got off the ship undetected.

When they got back to shore, Dalilah and Ray headed to the hospital to regroup. Perhaps Rickard would have some information on Gregori.

CHAPTER 70

GREGORI HAD ESCAPED from the Russian freighter through the smuggler's hole, used for maintenance purposes in modern times. He was still in amazing shape for a man his age. Despite the ocean tide, he managed to scuba back to the cabin with little effort.

Even though it was nighttime, he came slowly out of the water to check his surroundings. He assumed that the police had already finished their investigation at the house. He saw only a flashing yellow light in the driveway. Gregori moved silently toward the dunes to stash his duffel bag and gear in some brush.

A car was needed. The wrecker that was hooking up the van for transport to the police impound would do for now. He moved with stealth. Gregori came from behind the man, driving a blade deep into his throat. He slumped to the ground without a sound.

Gregori picked him up, dragged him to a nearby dune, and threw sand over him for a makeshift grave. He then retrieved the duffel bag and returned to the wrecker.

Something had gone wrong earlier, and he would find out who caused his plans to go awry. Someone would pay for this deviation. This was to be his last job before official retirement. No loose ends. His reputation was at stake.

CHAPTER 71

DALILAH AND RAY arrived at the emergency room of Carteret General Hospital. The waiting room was filled with uniformed police officers and special agents. Liza, Kyle and Brad had been moved into a large room together with Sarah, since she was obviously connected to the case. Police officers guarded the corridors and the exterior of the hospital. The officers pointed the way to the patients.

As they reached the room, Dalilah and Ray saw Special Agent Rickard wave for them to come in. Dalilah rushed into the room and shouted, "Mom, are you all right?"

"Yes, dear. I'm fine. I hear you did some pretty daring work to find me."

"Yes, but I had a little help. Dad's here."

Ray went to Liza's bedside. He hugged her and said, "It's great to see you, Liz."

"It's good to see you, too, Ray. Thank you for your help."

Ray looked at Kyle as Dalilah rushed to Brad's side. "Well, Kyle, I think you're gonna make it, friend."

"Yeah, and what about Gregori?"

"Well, he got away from us. We think he went to retrieve his drug shipment from the Russian freighter that was arriving in port. Somehow he got off the ship without our seeing him, so he may still be close."

Rickard piped, "Don't worry, I know his M.O. He's still in town, and we'll find him. He won't get away this time."

Dalilah wondered if Special Agent Rickard really knew this Gregori guy. The Russian was no amateur, and she hoped the rest of the task force understood this. She touched Brad's face as they looked at each other longingly. It was as if they were alone having a conversation without words. Then Brad broke the intimate silence.

"Did I hear you say 'mom'?"

"Yes, you did, Brad. I was going to tell you, but we sort of got busy. Liza is my mother. We maintain a professional cover for business purposes. Just like my name. It's really Elizabeth Kim. But you can keep calling me Dalilah."

"Well, you had me in the dark. Anything else I should know?"

"No, that's the big stuff. How are you feeling?" she asked. "Are you in pain?"

"No, right now I feel fine. They got the bullet out. The doc who patched me up said I should have lost more blood than I did. He said it was a miracle I survived. I didn't tell him about the Reiki."

"Good. He wouldn't understand it anyway. I'm so glad you're all right. And by the way, thanks again for saving my life. You Marine. Diving in front of bullets. Who do you think you are?"

Dalilah kissed Brad on the lips as Ray and Liza looked on. Brad had a very content look on his face.

CHAPTER 72

JOSEPH'S TEAM LEADER brought him up to date about Gregori's whereabouts. The security team had monitored police radio transmissions regarding anything about the Russian crime gang.

Joseph and his men drove through several checkpoints before arriving at Gregori's hideout. The house was dark, with crime scene tape surrounding the residence. One of Joseph's men found a body in the dunes. The corpse was covered in sand, but the killer hadn't cared if the body were found. It was obviously an unplanned kill.

The dead man's pockets were checked for identification. A wallet contained a business card with the name of a wrecker company. Joseph remembered passing a wrecker, yellow lights flashing, en route to the house. It had to be Gregori or one of his men.

Joseph radioed his other security teams and alerted them about the wrecker. He tried his best not to become emotional. Gregori had kidnapped his wife and thrown her into the ocean. His rage boiled as he pictured his wife covered in green gelatin and his son diving into the dark sea. If both of them had been lost, then he, too, would have been a lost man. He couldn't imagine his life without his wife and son. Gregori would pay for trying to take this gift away from him. He would pay with his life.

As Joseph conferred with a team leader, one of the other security teams radioed that a wrecker had been abandoned near the hospital. The truck still had a van in tow. Joseph ordered all teams on patrol to converge on the hospital. He also placed a call to his men inside the hospital to advise them of Gregori's possible presence.

***

At the back of the hospital, undetected, Gregori entered a door and made his way to the maintenance room. He found an identification badge on the desk and a maintenance worker's shirt on the chair. Gregori changed clothes and left the room.

CHAPTER 73

JOSEPH RAN INTO the hospital as soon as the SUV came to a stop. The police officers recognized him and allowed him to pass. He was relieved when he went to the large room and found Sarah and Ben sleeping safely. Joseph still had not shared his knowledge with the task force. He wanted to maintain anonymity as long as it kept his family safe.

Upon awakening, Sarah told Joseph she had spoken with the police. "I told them nothing except I was kidnapped by a man who told me Ben was hurt. Joseph, who is this Gregori they asked me about?"

***

The task force knew nothing specific at this point. As with most governmental agencies, cooperation was still a pipe dream. The mechanisms for total disclosure and sharing were not in place, which handcuffed police investigations. This was the most dangerous time for law enforcement officers since everything was in disarray. There was not enough information to formulate a larger picture. Many pieces to the puzzle had been found. Still no one knew the motive. No one knew Gregori's real mission and how determined he would be to accomplish it.

CHAPTER 74

GREGORI EXITED THE doctor's locker room. He had exchanged the maintenance uniform for a white lab coat, a more appropriate disguise. He had some loose ends to tie up, and he was determined to end his business career with a personal touch.

He entered the emergency room area. The police officers gave him only a cursory glance. After all, he looked distinguished and was dressed like a doctor. Gregori approached Liza's bedside and said, "And how are you feeling this evening, Liza?"

Liza's eyes widened when she saw Gregori. Before she could alert anyone, he removed a canister from his jacket pocket and pulled the pin. Everyone in the room looked up as he grabbed Liza around the neck and pulled her from the bed. Immediately Gregori's face was covered with red laser dots as police officers placed him in their sights.

Maintaining a cool disposition, Gregori said, "Gentlemen, if I drop this canister, everyone within ten square miles of this hospital will be dead in less than five minutes. I have in my hand a potent nerve agent, and I'm certain you're not prepared to kill so many people."

Gregori held the canister close to his body. He had rigged it with a fail-safe switch, commonly called a dead-man's switch. If he were shot or killed, the canister would fall, and the lever would break away to detonate. It would then signal a bomb he had put in the hospital's basement. The canister did not contain anything harmful, only smoke.

"Please holster your weapons, or none of us will go home tonight," Gregori said.

Rickard stepped up and stared at the Russian. "Now Gregori, you know there is no way out of here. Let Liza go, and we'll discuss your situation."

"You have nothing to offer me. I have my own plans, and I choose my way. Let me remind you, I am prepared to die. Are you? And are you willing to risk the lives of everyone here right now? You are only five minutes away from a painful death."

"Holster your weapons. Everybody do as he says," Rickard said.

Gregori smiled as his infiltration was complete. He looked at one of Joseph's team members and said, "Bring your boss, his wife and son here in front of me now."

The security officer hesitated.

"Don't make me ask again," Gregori said.

Rickard nodded, and the security officer pushed Sarah's hospital bed closer to Gregori. Joseph and Ben emerged from behind a wall of police officers. Joseph glared at Gregori.

"Have a seat, comrade Joseph," Gregori said.

Gregori released the grip on Liza's throat and patted her on the shoulder. Liza sat motionless as Gregori paced in small steps behind her. "Gentlemen, since I have your attention, I would like to set some facts straight. Do not think of me as a terrorist or as a horrible man hiding behind a woman hostage. Think of me as a capitalist with a business objective. I seek a profitable ending for all of us as we strive for a deal beneficial to us all. I have something you want, your freedom. And you have something I want, an audience of government officials. This is where your Mister Joseph Davidson comes into the picture. Or should I say Israeli intelligence officer Joseph Davidson?"

The police officers looked around at each other. Special Agent Rickard looked at Joseph and his family.

Gregori locked eyes with Dalilah. "Miss Smith, please come forward. I must admit I am surprised to see you. It is unfortunate that you were unable to complete your investigation. Your instincts were good. But our time frame was compressed, so we had to 'shake the tree,' as you say. And sorry if I scared you with the car chase. I was evaluating your professionalism under stress. You held up nicely."

Dalilah said nothing and stared at him.

Gregori returned the stare and said, "By the way, I hired you."

CHAPTER 75

GREGORI CHANGED HIS tone as he stared at Joseph. "Now for you, comrade. As a professional courtesy, I will tell you why you are here. If you search your memory, I'm sure you'll recall a car bomb in Cairo five years ago. Correct me if I miss any important details."

He looked at Sarah. "It was a Saturday, mid-afternoon. The marketplace was filled with tourists. A loud explosion sent car shrapnel in all directions. By day's end, thirty-four people had lost their lives. There were countless injuries and thousands of dollars of property damage."

Gregori focused on Joseph. "A call was made to the Egyptian government by an organization claiming responsibility. The organization was said to have been a local militant faction. However, we both know the real truth. It was you who killed all those people. It was you who killed my sister. She was on holiday. She was so innocent. I had given her that trip as a graduation present. In your scriptures does it not say 'an eye for an eye'? But I want more. I want to expose your operation to the American government."

Gregori looked around the room at the police officers, "You have an active Israeli intelligence officer working in your midst. He has been buying Russian diamonds and selling them as real diamonds. This money is for his black operations. He is a dealer in terror. Do you hear me, Joseph's wife and son? Your dear husband and father supplies money for people to be killed."

Ben looked at his father. Joseph maintained his composure. Sarah grabbed her husband's hand and squeezed it. He never said a word.

Suddenly, the curtain behind Gregori moved, and a flash of metal crushed his shoulder.

Kyle had been in the privy. He reached for Gregori's hand to stop the nerve gas from being deployed. They struggled for control of the canister. Kyle held on tightly as they fell to the floor. Gregori pulled away and the lever flew into the air.

A loud explosion convulsed the building as the main circuit panel in the basement blew apart. The lights flickered, and everyone panicked. Gunfire erupted. People dived for cover.

Kyle grabbed Liza and shielded her body with his as he held her tight to the floor. Ray fell as someone bumped into him. Brad purposely fell out of his bed and hit the deck. The emergency lighting came on as everyone looked around. The gunfire and Gregori's canister filled the room with acrid smoke.

No one was injured. Gregori was nowhere in sight. Joseph had disappeared. Sarah, Ben and the security team were also gone.

Ray was okay. Brad lay on the floor. Kyle was helping Liza. Ray stood and looked for Dalilah. The smoke made it difficult to see. "Dalilah!" he shouted.

CHAPTER 76

DALILAH BIT THE hand that covered her mouth. She could feel the leather glove between her teeth, so she clamped down harder until she felt flesh. The hand quickly released its grip. Before she could say a word, she heard Gregori's voice.

"Now, Miss Smith, if you make a sound, I'm sure they'll drug you, and I know you don't want that. Please cooperate with them, and they may let you go. They're using you only as insurance. After you've served your purpose, it's my guess you'll be set free."

"Gregori, you son of a bitch. I'm tired of your games. Do you have a problem with me?"

"You are a spirited one, Miss Smith. It's unfortunate we couldn't have worked together on a mutual mission. Perhaps in the future. But let me assure you it is not I who has arranged this little meeting."

Gregori held up his hands, and Dalilah saw him bound by handcuffs. "Perhaps you should ask the commandos why we are here."

Dalilah looked at the security team members in the van. No one was smiling. "Why have you taken me hostage, you assholes?"

None of the men said anything. They only stared at Dalilah. Each one had a semi-automatic weapon.

"Where are you taking me?"

Gregori spoke up. "I must say, Miss Smith, you are a unique individual, and I applaud you. You have shown a *joie de vivre* that I haven't seen in quite a while."

"Yeah, well, how about calling your goons and getting us out of here?"

"If only it were that easy, Miss Smith. In due time. I promise."

"And why did you hire me?"

"I knew about his smuggling. I didn't know his distribution system. That's where you came in. If I were to make inquiries, it would have set off a red flag. But you, a civilian, would be able to operate under the radar. Because of my employer's impatience, my timetable had to be altered. Don't worry, you will get your fee."

"What good is my fee if I'm dead?"

"Well, no matter now. Our lives are in the hands of Mr. Davidson."

Dalilah sat back and replayed the hospital scene in her head. *Apparently, Joseph didn't appreciate the soapbox Gregori had used to expose his operation. But why was I taken?*

A cell phone rang. The driver answered. He spoke in Hebrew, and she understood nothing. It was a short phone call. The driver made an immediate right turn.

She quieted her mind and focused on her dad. It was time to send a message. Hopefully, he was listening.

***

Only the emergency lights brightened the hospital hallways. The doors and windows were opened to vent the smoke. Special Agent Rickard and the other police officers searched the area, while Ray, Kyle and Liza stayed inside with Brad.

"Joseph's men had the automatic weapons. They were the ones firing," Ray said.

"Did anybody see Dalilah leave?" Kyle asked.

"No, when I got on my feet, I didn't see her anywhere," Ray responded.

Neither did Brad and Liza.

"With the roadblocks still up, they have to be in the city," Ray said. "I'm gonna try something and see if I can locate her."

Ray stepped into an empty room and shut the door. He took a couple of deep breaths and thought about Dalilah. Psychically, he would search the city in sections.

Time was of the essence, so Ray did a quick search geographically. The South seemed the strongest. He pictured Dalilah in his mind and called her name mentally. Then he focused on her face.

He could see water and a boat, maybe a yacht. Dalilah's energy felt agitated. He tried to clarify his feeling. She wasn't scared. She was pissed. That was it—Dalilah was pissed. That was a good sign.

CHAPTER 77

THE VAN STOPPED, and the doors immediately opened. Gregori was yanked out and thrown to the ground. One of the men helped Dalilah. The driver said, "Miss Smith, if you yell, you'll be shot."

Dalilah's fiery eyes were hot enough to burn a hole straight through him. A security officer grabbed her arm and directed her toward the dock. Two men escorted Gregori. They were at the marina, south of the city, where Joseph's yacht was moored. The engine was running and lights were on. Dalilah was told to get onboard.

Joseph came out of the cabin and said, "Welcome, Miss Smith. Please be seated."

Dalilah sat down and surveyed her situation. She heard another woman's voice, which she assumed was Sarah's, coming from the cabin below deck. Four security members guarded her topside.

Joseph and Gregori stepped into the bridge where two other security members were stationed. Dalilah could hear a heated discussion. She saw a security team member strike Gregori, and he fell to the floor. Dalilah thought, poor fellow. It couldn't happen to a nicer guy. Maybe this Joseph will be okay.

Ben came up from the cabin. "What was that thud?"

Dalilah motioned her head toward the bridge.

He looked at Gregori on the deck. Then he stared at Dalilah. "Why are you here?"

Joseph interrupted Dalilah's response. "Ben, do you need something? I asked you to stay below with your mother."

"No, I was just coming to ask if you needed help."

"No, not right now, son. Please tend to your mother."

Ben turned, looked apologetically at Dalilah and went below.

As far as Dalilah could determine, six security guards, Joseph, Sarah, Ben and Gregori were on the yacht. At least now she had a head count, and she could think about a plan of action. She looked around for anything she could use as a weapon. Joseph's security officers were not amateurs. They had searched her and found every weapon on her body. For now, she would play the pissed-off hostage. Patience would give her an opportunity to escape.

CHAPTER 78

RAY AND KYLE were by Liza's bed when Rickard entered the room and said, "I have some information on Joseph. We have three possible locations—his residence, business and a yacht at the marina. We have units on the way to all three places."

"Marina!" Ray and Kyle blurted.

Special Agent Rickard answered his phone. "Okay, there's nobody at the residence, and the business is deserted, too. He's got to be at the marina. That's the only way out of town for him. That might be where Gregori and Dalilah are. Do any of you know why Joseph would have taken Dalilah?"

"She must have some info about the diamonds," Ray said. "That's reason enough."

"Okay. I've got the SWAT team en route to the marina," Rickard said.

Ray looked at Brad. "Do you think your Coast Guard friend could help us locate Joseph's yacht?"

Rickard jumped in. "I'll make the call. This is a Homeland Security issue. You two get out there. A cutter will be standing by. Sergeant Lewis, what's your friend's name?"

Brad gave Rickard the information.

"Ray, Kyle, keep in touch," Rickard said. We've cleared the entire band, so any channel will work." He hurried from the room to catch the waiting helicopter.

Kyle patted Liza's hand. "Don't worry,"he said. "We'll get her back. Ray's already seen her, and she looked pissed. So you know what that means."

Liza smiled and gave Kyle a hug.

Ray went to Liza's side and hugged her. "Bring her back, Ray," Liza said with a trembling voice.

"Don't worry, Liz. We'll find her. It's not her time. I can feel it. We'll be back before you know it. Send her a message that we're on the way."

Ray and Kyle shook Brad's hand, then left the room. Kyle drove as Ray made a psychic connection with Dalilah. He sent her a message. We're coming, sweetheart. Be patient.

CHAPTER 79

JOSEPH ORDERED HIS men to take Gregori below. They had worked him over, so two men had to drag him down the stairs. Dalilah assumed the fun would continue with him.

"Miss Smith, if you would be so kind."

"I don't know anything, Joseph. What do you want with me?"

"We shall see, Miss Smith."

They took Dalilah to the galley where Gregori had been strapped to a chair. The room was exquisite with ornate decorations of Middle Eastern design. Dalilah looked for Ben and Sarah, but they were nowhere to be found. The yacht was evidently larger than it looked from the outside.

Joseph pointed to a chair. Dalilah would have a front-row seat to witness Gregori's interrogation. Four security members had come downstairs with Joseph, leaving the other two men topside. Dalilah kept track of everyone in case an opportunity presented itself.

Joseph opened a small metal attaché filled with syringes and drugs. The print was too small for her to read. Joseph tied a rubber band around Gregori's arm and thumped his elbow crease for a vein. He then removed a vial and filled a syringe. He pushed the plunger as the liquid squirted across the room, then injected it into Gregori's arm.

"It's too late for you, comrade," Gregori said. "No matter what I say, you're a dead man. You, your wife and your son. And it won't stop there. Your entire family. All dead. But the question is, who will kill you first? Your supervisors for your failure or my people for your interference?"

Joseph looked to his team leader and nodded. The man punched Gregori. Blood trickled from his nose. Joseph pulled the syringe from Gregori's arm and coldly said, "But you, comrade, will not be around to see it. That, I promise."

Gregori looked faint, and his breathing became erratic and shallow.

"Now, Mr. KGB," said Joseph, "that was a Mediterranean cocktail. A little something to help your heart and lungs. My people call it crucifixion without the cross. It's a very slow death. So enjoy."

"Watch carefully, Miss Smith. Hopefully, this will not be necessary for you, but that is your choice. Watch and learn. You cannot escape."

Dalilah stared at Joseph eye-to-eye without blinking. Her determination was showing in her disdain for this man. She didn't know who she wanted to kill first, Gregori or Joseph. Both were responsible for placing her mother in harm's way, and she couldn't forget what they'd done to Uncle Kyle and Brad. It was clear neither man had any regard for others. They were hell-bent on doing anything to achieve their goals.

She would be patient. All she had to do was wait. All real-life criminals, even professionals, make mistakes.

CHAPTER 80

GREGORI LOOKED WORSE after a few minutes. He mumbled unintelligibly. Joseph slapped him back to full consciousness.

"Now, Comrade Gregori, when was it you first discovered the components of my operation?"

Gregori refused to answer. The team leader zapped him with a stun gun. Fifty thousand volts of electricity shot through his body as he contorted and screamed.

"Now, Comrade, let me repeat the question in case you didn't hear it. When did you first know of my operation?"

"You stupid man!" Gregori shouted. "We have always known. Who do you think you're dealing with? We allowed you to use the bodies to smuggle our precious Russian diamonds. Do you think anything would leave Mother Russia without our knowledge?"

Joseph nodded and his security man zapped Gregori again.

"I know I'm a dead man," Gregori laughed. "But at least I will not have to watch my wife and son be killed in front of me."

The security man zapped him again, holding the stun gun against his skin for a long time. Gregori's eyes rolled up and into the back of his head. Joseph nodded and the man stopped. If he were unconscious, he would not feel anything. And Joseph wanted him to feel all the pain.

CHAPTER 81

"JUST FOR THE record," Joseph said, "and since you're dying, I'm the one who set up the operation in which your sister was killed. It wasn't my intention to kill civilians, only terrorists. That's the price of war."

Dalilah watched in amazement. This macho-male bullshit was driving her crazy. She found it difficult to stay calm. She looked around for things she could use as weapons. Two security members had gone topside. The other security man was behind her, so she decided it was time to be proactive. She planned to capture his attention while Gregori and Joseph battled back and forth. She was about to make a move when Ben entered. "Papa?"

"Ben. Please, Son, wait in the other room until I am finished. I must protect our family, and this is the only way I know how. Now, go to your mother!"

Ben's shoulders slumped as he went back into the other room. Joseph stopped with Gregori. "I'll be back shortly," he told the team leader.

This was the moment Dalilah had been waiting for. She stood up slowly and stretched her arms. "Just stretching, boys. It's been a long day."

Neither security man said anything. Dalilah bent over to stretch her legs and glanced behind her to see if the security officer were watching. He was staring at her ass, and that was what she wanted. She delivered a powerful rear kick into his knee and sent him to the floor in pain. The team leader attacked, but Gregori extended his foot and tripped him. Dalilah sidestepped him as he hit the floor hard. She retrieved his handgun and pointed it at them.

Joseph returned and saw Dalilah with the gun. She yelled, "Joseph, get in the corner with your men. Let's make this simple. I want off this boat, and you'll make it happen. I don't give a rat's ass what you do with Gregori. I figure he's got what's coming to him. But that's your little male bonding issue. I just want to go home!"

"You'll never get off the yacht alive, Miss Smith. I have four men topside."

"Yes, you do. But I have your family, and I assume you don't want any harm to come to them. After all, that's what all this bullshit is about. Right?"

As Dalilah spoke, a red laser dot appeared on her back. Through the skylight, a security officer topside aimed at Dalilah. Ben ran into the room. He saw the laser dot on Dalilah's back and jumped at her.

Joseph watched in horror as Ben dove toward Dalilah. Then the skylight exploded as the bullet penetrated the glass. The bullet tore through Ben's shoulder, and he and Dalilah fell to the ground.

"Ben, Ben! No!" Joseph screamed.

Sarah burst into the room. "Ben. No! Not my son."

Five security members crowded the galley as Joseph put a piece of cloth on Ben's wound. Dalilah wasn't hit, but two team members held her down.

"Get the first aid kit," Joseph ordered. "Now!"

Two security officers rushed to Ben's side. They applied bandages and monitored his vital signs. Ben did not move, and his breathing was erratic.

Gregori, still semi-conscious, smiled at Dalilah. "Miss Smith, I must say you have a way with men. How is it that they all dive in front of you to save you? You must share your secret with me."

Joseph looked at Gregori with disgust, but his hands were busy taking care of his son. Two men moved Ben to the adjacent room and placed him on a couch. His skin was clammy, and his face had turned pale. He was going into shock. Sarah was crying uncontrollably and mumbling in Hebrew as she watched her son die.

"I can help him," Dalilah offered. No one responded. "I said I can help Ben. Let me help him."

Sarah heard Dalilah and went to the galley. "Release her right now."

Joseph looked at Dalilah. "What do you mean, you can help him?"

"I'm a healer. Maybe you've heard of it. It's called Reiki. You may have heard it called something else, but the point is, I can help him."

"Miss Smith, need I remind you that if you do anything to harm my son, you will die a slow, painful death."

"Give me a break, Joseph. Your man shot him, not me. And besides, your son just saved my life. I owe him."

Sarah touched Joseph's arm. He nodded. "Let her go," he said.

Dalilah knelt beside Ben and placed her hands on his chest. She began meditating to quiet her mind. She really did owe Ben. She saw the river filled with logs and debris. She released all her thoughts, allowing them to float downstream until the river and her mind were clear. Then she imagined herself sitting at the lake's edge. No wind. Nothing but a crystal clear lake. Calm. Serene. Peace. She was ready. Dalilah kept her left hand on Ben's chest while she lifted her right hand in front of her. She moved her hand in circles, saying, "Cho Ku Rei, Cho Ku Rei, Cho Ku Rei." The power symbol opened a gateway for universal energy to flow through her. She placed both hands on Ben's chest. The room was quiet.

Dalilah's hands emitted a bluish-white glow as more of the Reiki energy passed through her. Everyone looked stunned as they witnessed the color coming from her hands. Joseph and Sarah prayed as they watched. The bluish glow soon surrounded Ben's entire body, consuming both him and Dalilah. They were connected in a cosmic sphere of Reiki energy.

In her mind, Dalilah spoke to Ben's higher self. Ben, come back to us. Thank you for saving my life.

You are a very noble person. Come back to us, Ben. Heal yourself. Allow the Reiki energy to heal your body. Your family is here. They love you, Ben. Come back to us.

Dalilah opened her eyes, and Ben coughed. Sarah cried as she saw the paleness leave her son's body. His Spirit was returning. Dalilah held Ben's shoulder for another fifteen minutes where the bullet had entered and exited, during which time Ben opened his eyes. Sarah moved closer, and he smiled at her. The bleeding had stopped. Joseph said nothing as he looked at Dalilah. Dalilah finished the healing and removed her hands. Ben grabbed her hands and held them tightly. He looked at Dalilah and said, "Thank you. I heard you. Every word. Thank you. Shalom."

Dalilah moved away from the couch as Joseph and Sarah attended to their son. One of the security officers moved in to grab Dalilah. "That won't be necessary," Joseph said. "Please see to it that Miss Smith has something to drink."

The security officer led her into the galley. As soon as he walked through the door, a heavy metal object crashed into the side of his head. He quickly fell and knocked Dalilah to the floor.

Gregori reached down and removed the pistol from his holster. Two other officers ran toward the galley, and shots were fired. Gregori stood in the doorway with a smoking gun. Both men had been shot in the head. Gregori leaned against the doorjamb and pointed the gun in the direction of Joseph, Sarah and Ben. He reached for the vials and injected himself with epinephrine to counteract the poison. Dalilah got up and kicked him from behind. He fell forward and hit the floor hard. The pistol flew out of his hand. She recovered the pistol and held it as Joseph stood. Now she had both Joseph and Gregori in the same room, and she held the gun.

Gregori laughed and made his way to a seat. "Yes, Miss Smith, you are quite a remarkable woman. Let's make a deal."

CHAPTER 82

DALILAH POSITIONED HERSELF with her back to the wall, away from any skylights. She watched the doorway in case Joseph's man on the bridge came down. She motioned for the security officers to take off their war gear and put their weapons on the floor. She wasn't going to take any chances. These were professionals. If she knew anything about securing a scene, this was the time to put theory into practice.

Thoughts streamed through her head. Dalilah took a deep breath and calmed down. The adrenaline was fading, and her hands stopped shaking.

As far as Dalilah could tell, the headcount was verified—two security officers in the room, two dead, one unconscious in the galley and one on the bridge. Joseph and Sarah were tending to Ben, who was conscious and doing quite well. Gregori, sitting in a chair, seemed to be more alert. Dalilah told one officer to drag the unconscious team member into the room. She removed his weapons and told them to do first aid. The two men checked his vitals and bandaged his head.

"Miss Smith," Gregori said. "I can get us out of here. Just one phone call, and we will disappear. You can go home and me, why, I can go on vacation. Just say the word."

Sarah looked at Joseph. He stood and approached Dalilah.

"That's far enough." Dalilah moved her firearm into a ready position.

Joseph backed away. "Miss Smith, you saved our son's life. How can I repay you for that? You have my word. Let us go. Let us get help for Ben, and you'll be free to live your life. You'll never see my family or me again. I promise and swear on all that is holy and on my son's life."

Gregori laughed and said, "Miss Smith, it seems that you have quite a dilemma. You have the power, and you have choice. You have both villains offering you freedom. Who will you trust?"

Dalilah looked around. Sarah stood. "Miss Smith, my son needs a hospital, and you want your freedom. You have my word that you will be set free. Isn't that true, Joseph?"

"Yes, you have our word."

Dalilah wanted to believe Sarah. But she was out in the middle of the Atlantic Ocean, holding a gun on international criminals. She took some deep breaths and then decided."Okay,you, captain of the guard, handcuff your man and the injured one," she said to the security leader.

He retrieved the handcuffs from each man's utility belt and placed them on their wrists.

"Now, lay him down on his side, and move him back to back with the injured guy."

The men complied. She then said, "Take the flexicuffs, tie their handcuffs together, and flexicuff their ankles together."

The man did as he was told.

Dalilah saw the surprised looks on their faces. "My dad is a retired police officer, if you're wondering. Now, team leader, you sit on the floor, and flexicuff your ankles together."

The man did as he was told.

"Put your hands behind your back, and lean against this post."

The security leader did as Dalilah demanded, and she handcuffed him to the post.

"Very efficient, Miss Smith," Gregori said respectfully.

Dalilah turned to Joseph. "Tell your man upstairs that we're headed back to town."

Sarah looked at Dalilah and said a silent thank you. Joseph picked up the radio and informed the security officer to adjust course back to the marina. He also informed the officer not to come below deck.

"Well, Miss Smith," Gregori sneered, "It seems things are working in your favor. What will you do with us when we get back to port?" Gregori inquired.

"We'll let the federal task force worry about the two of you."

Joseph stood to state his case. "Miss Smith, I assure you we have other options, should you care to explore them."

"Okay, Joseph, I'll bite. We have time before we get back to shore. What are the options as you see them?"

"You can delay your call to the authorities. Allow my family to leave so we can take our son to a hospital where discretion is prized. You will never see or hear from us again until you receive a phone call from Europe. I believe that seven figures deposited into a Swiss bank account in the name of your choosing should offset this inconvenience and misunderstanding."

Dalilah looked at Sarah. She saw sincerity in her eyes, and she believed Sarah would make sure this happened.

"Gregori, how about you?" inquired Dalilah.

"Of course! I have roughly ten million dollars in Russian diamonds, courtesy of Mr. Davidson, and another fifty million dollars of pure heroin in my duffel bag. How about I give you half, and you'll have my gratitude and protection from this day forward. You did in a way save my life. Because of your healing thing, I had time to escape. So I am in your debt."

"But Gregori, you tried to kill me. You shot Brad. You kidnapped Liza, and you beat up Kyle. How could I ever trust you?"

"Merely self-defense and operational protocol, Miss Smith. It was nothing personal. Plus, I didn't know you like I know you now. I live in a world full of geopolitical concerns, and those concerns are based on survival and financial prosperity. Not personal survival, but survival of a way of life for my family, friends and business partners.

"This is the real world, Miss Smith. Surely you're not naïve enough to believe this type of behavior does not perpetuate itself on a daily basis. And not just in our part of the globe. Look at your own country—death penalty, abortion, Iran-Contra, invasion of Iraq and Afghanistan, corporate fraud, arresting the poor while rich people go free, even for murder.

"All of us participate in these events, whether voluntarily or not. It's part of our world. I choose to accept the lot that I've been given, and I do what I can. Everyone in this room is an active participant of this grand charade of life. You, Miss Smith, are no exception."

"Nice soapbox, Gregori. Too bad you're full of shit. I happen to place a higher value on life. Life is not so cheap to me. Maybe I am naïve, but trust me when I say I believe in the basic goodness of people. And it's people like you who try to convince everybody that there is no goodness by traveling the globe with your pain-in-the-ass geopolitical concerns. How much stuff can one person have, anyway? How much is enough? What happened to just being a decent human being?"

"Miss Smith, you remind me of another very idealistic person, my sister. You know the story of my sister. Cairo, college graduate, bomb. Idealist meets the real world. And you know the results."

Joseph interjected softly, "You don't understand, Miss Smith. We don't know how to stop. It's all we know. We have been educated to think and act like this. It is our way of surviving—kill or be killed. You've heard the saying, 'the best defense is a good offense.' We're taught this in our schools and temples, through television and by our governments and politicians. It's difficult to think in any other way when you're immersed from birth into this way of life.

"Perhaps I can break the chain. It's too late for me, but I have my son to think about. He deserves a chance to live a peaceful life. And thank you again for saving his life. Your work will not go unrewarded. You have my word, no matter what you decide to do."

As Dalilah considered her options, the yacht came to a dead stop. "Joseph, what the hell is happening? I thought we were headed back to the marina."

Joseph radioed the bridge, but no one responded. A bright light flooded the room as Dalilah moved to a window. She saw a large vessel, white in color. A bullhorn sounded, "This is the United States Coast Guard. Prepare to be boarded."

Dalilah's heart soared. She was just happy it was all over. Sarah approached Dalilah and hugged her tightly. She lowered the pistol and embraced her.

Sarah whispered, "Thank you, Dalilah. You have an amazing gift. It is surely from God. Please use it often and wisely. We will be fine. Joseph will see to it. That's the type of man he is. He really is a loving husband and father. I want you to know that."

Dalilah looked at Joseph and Gregori. "If you two will try not to kill each other, I am going topside. I guess I won't have to choose after all."

Both men sat and said nothing. Dalilah went upstairs and disarmed the man on the bridge. She stood on the deck and waved at the Coast Guard cutter. As it moved closer, she saw her dad and Kyle waving back.

The yacht was boarded and flooded with Coast Guard personnel. Ben was airlifted to the hospital. Sarah was allowed to go with him. Joseph, Gregori and the security officers were brought up in handcuffs. The yacht would be towed in.

Dalilah ran to her dad and Uncle Kyle and hugged them both. "Looks like you had everything under control, sweetheart," Ray said proudly to his daughter.

Two body bags were brought up. Ray looked at Dalilah.

"I didn't do it. It's a long story."

CHAPTER 83

SPECIAL AGENT RICKARD basked in his newfound glory. His team had caught the infamous Gregori Petrolovich Novikov, renowned ex-KGB operative and major drug trafficker. Every alphabet agency in the world was looking for him—CIA, FBI, MI-6, MI-5, INTERPOL, German Intelligence and the French Government. Gregori had been on the international top-ten-most-wanted list for fifteen years. With him out of the picture, a multi-billion dollar drug cartel would be severely crippled. The heroin distribution for the United States would be cut by seventy-five percent.

Rickard was sure his promotion was in the mail. His perseverance had paid off. He imagined he'd be granted a post in D.C., perhaps as deputy director for the DEA. He even entertained a daydream of being the director. Why not? It could happen, he thought. Since part of the investigation had been cleared up, Rickard released members of the task force to return to their home bases.

Rickard submitted to the FBI's jurisdiction over Joseph, since he was a foreign intelligence agent. He was promptly taken to Langley, Virginia. Rickard assigned two agents to watch Sarah and Ben at the hospital. Ben was expected to make a full recovery thanks to Dalilah.

A State Department official arrived from Washington, D.C., to take care of Gregori. After two hours of interrogation, he was whisked away in a black helicopter. Somebody wanted him badly. Rickard was unable to find out who pulled the strings.

***

Dalilah had watched as Gregori was escorted to the helicopter. He smiled at her. Not a weird smile, but more of a friendly, see-you-later smile.

Ray, Kyle and Liza had been allowed at the debriefing when Dalilah reported her version aboard the yacht. She told the whole truth as she remembered it. The investigator told her Gregori's account matched hers exactly. The task force investigators said they were impressed with her performance.

Dalilah met with Brad after finishing her reports. She told him she'd return as soon as the case was cleared up in Greensboro. She promised some tender loving care. Brad told her he would be released in two days.

After a day of debriefing, Dalilah boarded a helicopter with her dad, Kyle and Liza. Dalilah and her dad sat beside each other and embraced in the special way only a father and daughter could.

"You did some fabulous work, kid. Think about continuing your training. I think you're ready now. Don't you?" Ray said.

"Yeah, maybe, Dad. I need a vacation. But I do admit I remembered more than I had thought possible. It's like I just knew it. I didn't have to think about it. It was inside me. I had to trust myself. And I want you to know I heard your voice a lot. You were in my head—all the memories, all the training, the martial arts, the Reiki, the meditation philosophy, it was all in me.

"So, I know I may have seemed ungrateful at the time for the teachings, but I do want to thank you with all my heart and soul. Most of all, thank you for having faith in me and my abilities."

"That's what parents do, Elizabeth. You truly are a special woman. Never forget that. And no father could be prouder of his daughter than I am. You kept your cool under the worst possible conditions, and you survived. You did what you had to do in the heat of battle, and you survived. I love you, sweetheart."

Dalilah and her father continued embracing. Maybe she would take her dad up on the training aspect. A little more spiritual training couldn't hurt, she thought.

Dalilah moved across to hug her mom. Liza held her tight against her chest. They looked into each other's eyes and communicated without having to say a word.

Dalilah felt the drain of the experience. The adrenaline rush was gone, and the sound of the rotor blade was hypnotizing. She was sleepy. She laid her head on her dad's shoulder and drifted into a much-needed nap.

CHAPTER 84

TWO WEEKS HAD passed since the conclusion of the case. Even though Gregori had been the client in this case, he had paid the fee up front to the information broker. He had called the broker to relay his satisfaction. Dalilah received full compensation for her investigation.

She had discovered a covert heroin distribution network using the same methods to deliver its products to the United States. Furthermore, she had exposed a foreign intelligence undercover operation. Her name was mentioned in some high level briefings with federal agencies. But the government didn't offer a reward for her last two contributions. As a bureaucrat sermonized from his elitist high ground, "It was your patriotic duty as an American citizen."

Liza recovered fully and was back in the office within two days. Dalilah noticed she and Uncle Kyle were hot and heavy. She even felt they would be married soon.

Dalilah received a postcard from her dad in Hawaii. He was finishing his spiritual retreat with Jeanne. Ray and Jeanne would stay in Hawaii for another three months, according to the postcard.

Brad and Dalilah spoke on the phone every day. He was adjusting as well as could be expected for an ex-Marine. Healing always happens too slowly from the warrior's perspective. He was cleared for light-duty work, so he kept a presence in the office. He would be promoted to lieutenant the following month. The Marine Patrol was impressed with the part he had played in the federal investigation. He was also offered a position with the Department of Homeland Security. Brad told them he would think about it during his recovery.

Dalilah left the office early to go home and pack. She planned to see Brad this weekend. She also needed to tidy up a bit. After her experiences, house cleaning was not a priority. She thought about getting a maid like Laura had. The mail had piled up on her dining table, and she couldn't stand the clutter.

She brewed some chai tea and looked for a snack. All she found was an old bagel and some cream cheese. She settled for that and sat down. As she sipped her tea, Dalilah checked her phone messages. The first one was from Uncle Kyle.

"Dalilah, sweetheart, this is Uncle Kyle. You may want to sit down. That son of a bitch Gregori has been given diplomatic status, which means all his criminal actions have been exonerated under diplomatic immunity. He was deported yesterday to Russia. I just got off the phone with Rickard who's very upset. Same thing for Joseph. He was a security attaché at the D.C. embassy. Don't know where he is. Kinda sucks I know. Oh well, just thought you'd like the update. And by the way, how about being your mother's maid of honor? Give us a call when you can. We'll both be at my place. Love you."

Dalilah stared at her tea and bagel. She couldn't believe Gregori was going to walk. I should have shot the bastard when I had the chance! And Joseph, too. She pondered the justice system when the doorbell rang. The UPS man gave her two small, padded manila envelopes.

Inside the first package was a black velvet bag. She untied the knot and dumped the contents onto her plate. She couldn't believe her eyes. The plate was filled with hundreds of diamonds in all sizes and shapes. Some of them had fallen onto the floor and into her lap. She excitedly opened the sealed white envelope and read the message.

Miss Smith,
I must say you are indeed a remarkable woman. Please allow this to be a token of my admiration. You did inadvertently save my life. Joseph would have terminated me if you hadn't saved his son. Who knows what the future holds. Perhaps we will cross paths soon.
Sincerely, G
P.S. Hope you like the Russian diamonds. Selling price—about $1,000,000.

Dalilah studied the package for a return address. She was sure Gregori had covered his tracks. She had no idea what to do with the diamonds. She had been given bonuses before, but not from someone like Gregori. Laura would know what to do. For now, Dalilah would keep them in her gun safe.

Dalilah sat in her chair again, gathered her thoughts and sipped her tea. She looked at the other package, deciding whether or not to open it. Its return address was from Switzerland, but no name was indicated. Maybe it was from Laura. Dalilah hadn't heard from her since she'd moved. She opened the envelope and found two smaller white envelopes. The envelopes were labeled #1 and #2. Dalilah opened the one marked #1 first.

> Ms. Smith,
> Ben is doing just fine, and he'll be back on his feet in no time. He says to tell you hello. Thank you for saving his life. How can we ever repay you for what you did for him? You have a wonderful gift. Thank you for sharing it with us. We are honoring our promise.
> Shalom, Joseph and Sarah
> P.S. Call the number in envelope #2. Use the password and code verifier as it is listed. You have thirty days to activate your account.

Dalilah was stunned. It was as if Joseph and Gregori had coordinated their letters. Dalilah sipped her tea and tried to remain calm. She knew there was a vast time difference in Geneva, and she considered waiting until tomorrow. But her curiosity got the best of her.

A woman with a French accent said, "Good evening. May I please have your activation code?"

"Yes. 105114145."

"One moment, please. Is this Miss Dalilah Smith of Greensboro, North Carolina, United States of America?"

"Yes, it is."

"Please authenticate, Miss Smith."

Dalilah searched the paper for the other number. "The number is 411291218-19139208."

"Yes, Miss Smith, you have authenticated properly. Now, how may I be of service?"

"I just received my papers today. Could you tell me what services are available?"

"You may check balances, transfers, withdrawals or other account activity."

"Okay, how about all of those."

"Yes, Miss Smith. Just one moment . . . for the past thirty days, you have had a fund transfer and deposit of two million dollars US. You have had no withdrawals or other activities within the past thirty days. And your balance with interest as of the close of business today is two million, thirty thousand dollars US."

Dalilah sat silent. Her mind went somewhere to parts unknown. The sound of the woman's voice brought her back to her body.

"Is there anything else, Miss Smith?"

"No. Yes. How can I make a withdrawal?"

"You may go to your local bank, and the money will be wired into your account locally. Just have your authorization and activation code when you make the withdrawal inquiry."

"Yes, thank you."

"And thank you, Miss Smith."

Dalilah hung up and sipped her tea while her mind sorted all the details into manageable compartments. Diamonds, Swiss bank accounts, activation and authentication numbers, secret packages and global politics. What a difference a day could make! She was living proof that life continues giving and people must ride the wave or the wave will ride them.

Dalilah gathered her senses, but she felt a certain nervousness welling within her. She opened the end-table drawer next to her and removed a stale pack of Virginia Slims menthols. She needed some grounding, and sometimes a cigarette was the only way. She lit up and tried to relax.

She was too excited, but who could she tell? She thought she should keep this quiet for a while, but she would have to tell someone. She really didn't know if any of this were legal. But what the hell, the system had let Gregori loose, and apparently Joseph, too. So she wouldn't feel obligated to inform anyone, especially the authorities, about the packages.

When Dalilah glanced at her mail, a particular letter captured her attention. It was from the Diamond Consortium of New York. She opened the envelope.

> Miss Dalilah Smith,
>
> In reference to the diamond you submitted for testing, we must inform you that with 99.95% accuracy, its origin is Russian Phyanite, a synthetic diamond. Please refer to your local jeweler for further details or call us at 1-800-DIAMOND.

It had been a gift of love. They were both young, but in love. Her parents had disagreed with her choice to marry. Too young they said. She thought it would last forever. And now, divorced, she knew better. That son of a bitch gave me a fake diamond. He said it was real. He promised.

Dalilah tore the necklace from her neck. She took a deep draw from her cigarette. Smoke came out of her nose.

Now, she was grounded. Now, she was pissed!

AUTHOR'S NOTES

History of Reiki

Mikao Usui of Kyoto, Japan, rediscovered Reiki at the end of the 19th century. He named the energy Rei-Ki—universal life energy. Reiki has roots in Buddhism, Qi Gong and Shinto.

Mikao Usui was born August 15, 1865, in southern Japan. He often traveled to a Buddhist temple on Mount Kurama in northern Kyoto. This ancient temple had roots in Tibetan Buddhism. Once while standing under the waterfall on Mount Kurama, he had a satori—a sudden understanding. During a twenty-one-day fast, he experienced the Reiki power.

After that experience, he founded the Usui Reiki Ryoho Gakkei—Usui Reiki Healing Method

Society. It is believed that Mr. Usui taught Reiki to approximately two thousand people.

Mr. Usui died at the age of sixty-two on March 9, 1926. He was buried at Saihoji Temple in the Tokyo suburbs.

Dr. Chujiro Hayashi

Mr. Usui trained Dr. Chujiro Hayashi in 1925. Dr. Hayashi was given permission to teach and train his own students. He operated a healing dojo. In 1938, he initiated one of his students, Hawayo Takata, as a Reiki Master.

Hawayo Takata

Ms. Hawayo Takata received her Reiki Master initiation on February 22, 1938. She is credited with bringing Reiki to the United States. She lived in Hawaii and initiated twenty-two Reiki Masters before her death on December 11, 1980.

***

Reiki has evolved into a myriad of hand positions, levels/degrees and attunement ceremonies. There are many variations of Reiki, since it readily complements other wellness modalities. It is recognized worldwide as a natural healing method. As societal ideas of wellness and health continue to expand, so will Reiki.

The Five Reiki Principles

The Meiji Emperor of Japan (1868–1912) established principles for living a fulfilled life. The principles were established in an effort to increase personal happiness, as well as the happiness of others.

The Emperor honored Sensei Usui for his good deeds. Sensei Usui adopted the Emperor's five principles for Reiki:

1) Don't get angry today.
2) Don't worry today.
3) Be grateful today.
4) Work hard on your spiritual self today.
5) Be kind to others today.

Cho Ku Rei

(Say 3x.)
"By Divine Decree"

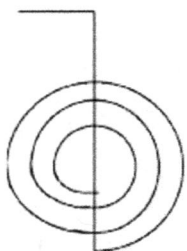

Medicine Buddha Mantra

Tayatha Om, Bekhaze, Bekhaze,
Maha, Bekhaze, Bekhaze,
Raja, Samugate, Soha.

Phonetic

Tie yah thah Aum, Bey kah zay, Bey kah zay,
Mah ha, Bey kah zay, Bey kah zay,
Rah Jzah, Sah moo gah tay, So ha.

Translation

In such a manner as follows – (Tayatha)
Seed syllable of the Body of Buddha – (Om)
Medicine, healing, cure – (Bekhaze)
Medicine, healing, cure – (Bekhaze)
Great – (Maha)
Medicine, healing, cure – (Bekhaze)
Medicine, healing, cure – (Bekhaze)
King – (Raja)
Crossed the Ocean of Samsara – (Samugate)
Receiving the blessings of all Buddhas – (Soha)

RESOURCES

- United States Coast Guard: www.uscg.mil/
- North Carolina Marine Patrol:
www.ncfisheries.net/ncdmf/patrol/index.htm
- www.EarthStarSpiritualCenter.org